THE

Unlikely Story

OF A **PiG** IN THE

City

THE
Unlikely Story
OF A PiG IN THE
City

Jodi Kendall

HARPER
An Imprint of HarperCollinsPublishers
Peachtree

Library of Congress Control Number: 2017943444
ISBN 978-0-06-248453-6

Typography by David Curtis
17 18 19 20 21   CG/LSCH   10 9 8 7 6 5 4 3 2 1

First Edition

For Leslee,
my first reader, since the beginning.

Chapter 1

RUNT RESCUE

Hamlet arrived on Thanksgiving Day, all pink and squirmy and perfect in my brother's football arms, while my dad stacked a pile of smoked bacon on his plate.

"Not a chance," Dad said, pointing at Tom with a silver fork. "Pigs don't belong in the city."

"But Dad—" Tom's voice cracked. It always broke like that when he was upset but didn't know how to say it, as if feelings somehow tickled his throat.

"I want it *out*."

The sound of the crispy bacon snapping between Dad's teeth was a gavel. It meant we couldn't keep Hamlet. It meant she was destined for death.

Tom made the rounds of staring everyone down. We were all squashed around the family table, my parents on each end, and my younger sister, Amelia, next to me—as if she'd sit anywhere else—and my older sisters Ellen and Sarah across from us, where they'd been fighting over bumping elbows and who got a bigger portion of stuffing. But that was before Tom showed up—late, as usual, although this time for a reason that wasn't just football.

If it weren't for the piglet, I wouldn't even look at Tom. Every time he came home from school it was another reminder of how tall us Shillings are destined to be—Tom could reach the ceiling with his fingertips if he tried. I took a bite of Mom's homemade cranberry sauce, and the sour taste mirrored how I felt deep down inside.

Tom adjusted Hamlet in his arm cradle. She let out a high-pitched, earsplitting squeal that made Sarah scowl and cover her ears with her hands. My brother might have a big old softie heart, but he didn't know animals. Not like I did, at least. He wasn't even holding her right. I'd never held a pig before, but I knew I could do it better than he could. I set down the pepper grinder, ready to leap up and take her from him, but Mom met my eyes and gave a little shake *no* with her head.

"I can't take the pig back," Tom said. "I sorta . . . you know . . . stole it and all."

Dad's fork clanged against the edge of his plate. "What do you mean you *stole* it?"

"Well, it was more like *taking* it. We were at Natalie's parents' farm, and there were too many piglets in the litter, and this one wasn't strong enough to really squirm in and get milk from the mom pig. Natalie said that as the other piglets grow, they bully the runts out of the way until—until . . ." Tom's voice trailed off dramatically, letting us imagine what might have happened to her. "She was so scrawny and sad and just *moments* away from death, so I rescued her. Actually, Dad, the real question here is whether or not I'm a hero!"

Ellen glanced up briefly from the pages of her book, a smirk on her face. Mom touched her hand to her chin. "How long exactly have you had the pig, Tom?" she asked my brother.

He beamed. "Twenty-four hours. Snuck her into my dorm room in my football helmet." At that moment, the piglet shifted in my brother's arms, letting out a series of oinks and grunts.

Dad pursed his lips together. "Should I be expecting a phone call from the school about this?"

Tom grinned, all teeth and charm. "No worries, Dad. We just left Nat Geo Wild on the TV while we took our midterms, and Hamlet felt right at home. Our hall monitor never noticed she was there!"

Ellen looked up again from her book. "Hamlet?"

"Oh—yeah, that's her name. My floor voted on it and Hamlet beat out Oinkment, Hogwash, and Kevin Bacon."

"I would've picked Kevin Bacon," said Sarah.

"I see." Dad had no trace of emotion in his voice. "Tom, litter runts aren't supposed to make it. That's called natural selection."

"Let's keep the pig! It'll be our pet, like Sugar," Amelia said, her eyes widening at the idea. "It can stay in my room!"

Like Dad would ever let us keep a pig. Didn't Amelia know that? She was eight years old now, but sometimes I swear she acted like a kindergartener!

"You mean *our* room," Sarah said, "and no." Sarah was fifteen, a freshman in high school, and had more attitude than anyone I knew.

"Josie, don't feed Sugar table food. You're turning her into a beggar," Dad said. I made a face and gently pushed the dog's wet nose away from my plate. "Take the pig back, Tom. It's not up for discussion."

"But I can't—*the farm is two hours away from the city!*— and the game tonight!" Tom's voice rose again.

Dad sighed. He looked at Mom. "Emily—is this something you can help out with? I'm on deadline here."

Mom was staring at the piglet, as if she wasn't sure whose side she was on yet. Finally, she shook her head. "I'm not missing the football game, if that's what you're suggesting, Stephen." It's true—she never missed one of Tom's games. His college was about thirty minutes away, and while home games were always a big deal, a night game on Thanksgiving was *huge*.

"Besides. We agreed no work on holidays, deadline or not, remember?" Mom clamped down on a slice of white meat with the turkey tongs, setting it down on my plate. Then she reached for a ladle. "Gravy?"

I don't even eat meat anymore. It started because my best friend Lucy and I made a bet that I'd go vegetarian until Christmas. She didn't think I could do it, but I was three months in already, and I wasn't about to lose forty dollars. Soon I'd need that money for new grips for gymnastics. Plus, I'm no cheater.

"No, Mom," I said. "I've told you a million times,

I'm a vegetarian now."

"You need your protein, honey."

"There's protein in beans," I argued. "At least I think there is. Right, Ellen?" I glanced over at my older sister for confirmation, but she was back to reading again and ignored me.

"The pig stinks. Can I be excused now?" asked Sarah, scowling. "I've lost my appetite."

"Tom, can't you just call someone to pick the pig up?" Dad suggested.

"I tried. . . . It's a holiday. No one's picking up the phone. *Ow!* Hamlet! Her hooves are digging into my jersey . . . can I put her down?" Tom always wore his jersey on game day—a superstition or something.

Dad wasn't ready to give in. "No. Did you post an ad on the internet?"

Tom wrinkled his nose. "You guys got internet after I left?"

I almost laughed. Fat chance of that happening either. We were probably the only family in the city without cable and internet. Dad said that using the "public library's services" worked just fine for our needs. I exchanged a look with Sarah, who had secretly hacked into Mrs. Taglioni's Wi-Fi network next door months ago so she could check her email on the family computer.

Dad rubbed his temples. "It's Thanksgiving! Ellen, please put the book away. Josie, it's about time you quit this ridiculous vegetarian bet. No, Sarah, you are not excused until we're all finished. Amelia—enough with the cranberry sauce already, or you'll be sick. *Can't we just finish our meal in peace?*"

Ellen snapped the book closed. She traced her finger along the bright yellow dragon across the cover and said cheerfully, "I missed the family vote. Are we keeping the pig?"

"We're NOT keeping the pig."

Dad's voice startled Hamlet, and she oinked so loud that Sugar perked up her ears. Animals might not talk, but they can understand feelings just the same, that much I knew. Some things are instinct.

The more I watched the piglet burrow her snout against my brother's neck, the more I felt bad for her. She was just an innocent little creature. If Hamlet were sent back to the farm, she'd die. But Dad's rules were firm and final. . . . What was I supposed to do?

Hamlet tried to wriggle out of Tom's grasp again, her little hooves digging into his arms. I was ready to burst from my seat, but Mom's watchful eyes held me back for the second time. I didn't want to get in trouble. I couldn't get grounded now, not when I just had gotten to Level 5, and my first big gymnastics meet was around the corner.

But Hamlet squealed at the top of her piglet lungs, and it felt like both of us couldn't take it anymore. She wanted out of Tom's arms, and I wanted out of this seat. I pushed back my chair, its pinewood feet grinding rails into the carpet, and lifted Hamlet from his arms.

"Geez, Josie," Tom said. "You're nearly as tall as I am now. You up for playing catch later?"

I hunched my shoulders and cradled Hamlet close. Like I'd ever play catch with Tom. My palms were calloused enough from learning the new uneven bars routine.

Besides, I couldn't risk a broken finger.

"Josie's like a foot taller than Lucy now!" piped in Amelia.

I glared at her. "Not a foot."

Sarah smirked. "I'm not sure I can call you Shortcake anymore."

"I call next to hold Hamlet!" Amelia raised her hand in the air.

"No one should be holding the pig." Dad's ears now burned a deep red. "Farm animals carry all sorts of diseases."

The piglet snorted and nestled against the crook of my neck, hiding behind my brown hair. I couldn't help but smile. I'd seen pigs up close before on a class field trip, and I'd heard the sounds they made, but I was surprised by how Hamlet smelled like fresh cedar chips. She smelled *clean*.

A tremble roared through Hamlet's body. Her fine, white-colored hairs stood on end, and I stroked them down, whispering into her twitching ears. "There, there, Hamlet," I whispered. "Everything will be okay. . . . Now you just sit right here." I gently placed her down in front of the air vent. She curled into a little half-moon position, her skin turning warm from the shock of heat filtering into our dining room. She was mostly pink in color, with some light gray spots across her back.

"Tom," Dad started, his voice low and calm. "Go scrub your hands with antibacterial soap and come back here and eat. You need your energy for tonight's game." Then he turned to me. "Josie, put that pig in the doghouse out back, clean up, and finish eating with us. Your mother and I will discuss what to do with it when we're done."

"Her name is Hamlet," I said, my shaky words barely audible. "Not *it*."

Dad reached for the cranberry sauce. "You shouldn't name the animal. It'll only make it harder to say good-bye later."

A knot formed in my throat. I didn't argue with him often because it seemed pointless. No one listened to me in this family anyway. I was almost at the bottom of the food chain. Average at everything. Nearly invisible.

"If Tom keeps the pig, I want a horse," said Sarah.

"You're not getting a horse." Mom shook her head. "Our backyard is barely big enough for the grill."

"And my bike," added Amelia.

"We could board it—"

"Wait, it's not *my* pig," Tom interrupted, coming back to the table. He took a heaping spoonful of stuffing and said with a full mouth, "I've got football!" He said it like we didn't know. Like it wasn't always about being a starter for his university team and his whole obsession with the championship season.

Sarah glared at Tom. "Nice earring."

Tom's spoon fell from his hand to the carpet. He quickly brushed the longer ends of his hair over his ears. But it didn't do much. Now that Sarah said it, it was obvious—something round and small sparkled in the middle of his right lobe.

"You got your *ear pierced*?" Dad fumed.

POUND! POUND! POUND!

The sound was a hard knock against our dining room wall. We knew that sound all too well: our neighbor, cranky old Mrs. Taglioni, always pounds on it when we get too loud.

Dad cleared his throat and said more calmly and quietly, "Let me see that earring."

Tom picked up his fallen spoon, dusting it off with a napkin. Then he dusted off Dad's comment by saying, "Whoa, whoa, guys. I think we're losing sight of the real problem here. What *in the world* are we going to do with Hamlet? I mean, a pig in the city! Whoever heard of such a thing?"

I stretched out next to Hamlet on the floor, peeled the fleece socks off my feet, and rubbed my toes into the dining room carpet. Even though it was Thanksgiving and I should be giving thanks for everything, inside I just didn't feel thankful. All I wanted was a break from my family. There were always people in my space and voices arguing in my ears. And the Ohio winter was just starting to roll in. There'd be months and months of shoveling snow from the front stoop, having nothing else to wear but Sarah's ratty sweaters from last year, and waiting at the bus stop while my lips shriveled up like raisins in the crisp air while all my friends got rides from their parents. Not that I wanted my parents to drive me in our embarrassing beat-up van, either, with its big white stripe and strange rattling noise.

And at Henderson Middle School, I felt like an outsider, too. I only had a few friends from the block who went there, and this year I had just one class with Sully and another with Fernanda. I barely even saw Carlos unless we were hanging out on the stoops. It seemed like everyone at school already had friend groups and I just wasn't a part of them. How do you make friends with people who don't want to get to know you?

Outside of school, most of my free time was spent with my gymnastics team, but none of my teammates went to dumpy HMS. They went to fancy private schools, which, of course, we couldn't afford.

All I had that was just *mine* was gymnastics—and every year, with every inch I grew, I felt even that slipping away from me. It was getting harder to launch my body from the mat into a perfect glide kip on the uneven bars. I could land a back walkover on the beam, but my balance was off, and the more I worried about it, the more I wobbled. I tried to get stronger in practice, but I only felt more awkward, unable to determine how much power I needed to stretch to reach or leap to land. My body was tricking me, and just when I figured it out, I seemed to grow another inch, and my form turned sloppy all over again. And I wasn't the only one noticing.

I closed my eyes, trying to listen only to the sweet piglet sounds coming from beside me on the floor. I wouldn't think about what Coach said. Not now. Not *ever.*

Hamlet's body shifted beneath the palm of my hand, her legs stretching out against the heating vent on the wall. She slept a lot like Sugar did, on her side, with her head tilted back. Sugar had retreated to the living room a long time ago. She'd gotten over her initial curiosity about Hamlet. My gaze shifted to my family, sitting around the table. It seemed like they all had, too. If it were up to them, Hamlet would be *ham*—and that was her destiny if I didn't stand up for her.

"Mom, Dad . . ." I started, but I stopped when tears glazed across my eyes. If I told them my idea, I was positive they'd say no. But now that I'd held Hamlet, I felt connected to her. I couldn't let them get rid of her.

My parents ignored me. Mom cut her turkey up into perfectly sized cubes while Dad took another swig of iced tea. "Hello?" I tried again, more firmly this time, but soft enough that my parents wouldn't get angry at my tone. "Mom and Dad, please *listen* to me! She can't go to a farm that will kill her. She's only a baby pig. Hamlet has lots of life left in her."

Dad sighed. "That's what pigs are for, Josie. They're raised for meat."

Hamlet licked my knuckles. "Not this one," I whispered, leaning over to hug the piglet. Then, with more courage, "I'll find her a home, okay? Just give me some time, and I'll find someone who wants her as a pet."

Mom watched Hamlet burrow against my neck, and her eyes softened. "Stephen, perhaps we should talk about this. Maybe Josie has a good idea?"

"It's really not," Ellen said, reaching for a shiny hologram bookmark on the table. "Having a pig in a city isn't practical. And it's not fair to the animal."

"Plus it's gross," added Sarah.

"I'm glad I'm not the only rational one in this family," grumbled Dad.

I felt my heart rate skyrocket, the way it always does

when I'm outnumbered in a family vote. I had to do something. Fast. "Mom, Dad, please—just give me until New Year's," I blurted. "I'll find her a home by then. Promise."

"That's a *whole month* away, Josie." Dad clasped a hand over his heart like the idea of living with a pig was physically painful. Then Dad gave my brother a hard look. "And Tom, you're not off the hook with that earring. Your mother and I will discuss that later."

"At least it wasn't a tattoo," Tom said, reaching for another slice of turkey with his bare hands. "Turkey, Josie?"

I glared at him. My brother's the king of changing the subject.

"A whole month outside is much too cold for a baby animal," said Mom, her hand raised to her chin again. "What about that little nook under the stairs? We could move the bookshelf out of the way, maybe lay down some old newspapers. I'm sure Ellen has leftovers from last weekend, don't you, Ellen? That would make a nice little temporary home for him."

I didn't dare correct Mom that Hamlet was a *her* not a *him*. I liked the idea just fine.

"I'll move the bookshelf!" I volunteered.

"Josie, do you even know what pigs eat? And who's going to pay for its food?" Dad crossed his arms over his chest. "Sugar's dog food is over thirty dollars a bag."

I bit my lip. I hadn't thought of that. I'd been saving my measly eight-bucks-a-week allowance money for a while now, because I knew it was coming—the day Mom and Dad would make me quit the gymnastics team because we couldn't afford it anymore. Then I'd have to start paying dues on my own. I didn't want to quit. Gymnastics was *everything* to me.

"I have allowance money saved," I said. Plus, I was *this* close to winning the bet with Lucy, so that'd be a little extra. Hamlet snuggled against my leg. "I can help pay for her food."

"You're wasting your breath, Shortcake." Sarah's mouth was full of food, but I could hear her attitude crystal clear. "It took us six months to convince Dad to adopt a dog. He barely even pets Sugar, and she's like ancient now."

"I prefer Sugar's company from afar." Dad scooped up mashed potatoes with his spoon. "And pigs are dirtier than dogs. Josie, please go wash your hands—and besides, I'm not sure an eleven-year-old is ready for the responsibility of rearing a *farm animal*—"

"I'm almost twelve," I broke in. "And don't forget I'm the one who walks Sugar most of the time. It's just a month. Then Hamlet will be gone. I promise!" I crossed my fingers behind my back.

"Actually, thirty-eight days to be exact," corrected Ellen, the know-it-all. "That's over a month away."

More time to convince them why we should keep the piglet.

Perfect!

"I help walk Sugar!" Amelia protested, plunking a fork into her heaping pile of fluff stuff. It's what we call this dish that Mom makes with chopped grapes and walnuts and whipped cream, and it's everyone's favorite side dish on Thanksgiving. So if you don't scoop your serving right off the bat, no one's saving it for you. That's how it is in big families. You have to take what you can get.

I scratched behind Hamlet's ears. She was just a runt piglet trying to stay alive in a family with a ton of kids. We had that in common.

Dad sunk into his seat. He made eye contact with my mom. "Emily?" he said, without stating the question.

She smiled at him, then at me. "I think it's a good idea."

Dad sighed. He stared for what felt like forever, sizing me up like he does football players at Tom's games. "Okay," he finally said.

From across the room, Tom gave me an air high five. I grinned.

"We saved Hamlet! We saved Hammmmmmmlet!" Amelia cheered. "We're going to be the coolest family on the block!"

"Doubt that," grumbled Sarah, pushing her blond hair from her face.

"This will be a disaster," predicted Ellen.

"We trust you, Josie," Mom said, nodding my way.

"And whatever the pig does is on your shoulders, Josie," Dad warned. "You're responsible for everything she needs: exercise, food, cleaning. And I mean *everything*. If that pig so much as sniffs my slippers, I'm turning her loose."

I nodded. Dad would never turn her loose in the city—he's much too sensible for that. But he *would* give the pig away to a bacon farm, and I had exactly thirty-eight days to convince my parents why we should keep her.

My heart swelled with excitement. This was gearing up to be the best holiday season of my life, even though

I was still stuck in central Ohio, hadn't nailed my back tuck yet, and felt squished like a sardine in this tiny jam-packed house.

But what I *did* have was Hamlet.

I'd never thought about having a pet pig before today—and suddenly, I couldn't imagine life without her. I couldn't wait to bathe and feed her, introduce her to my friends, walk her around the yard, and snuggle up on the couch watching holiday movies.

The little piglet nestled up against my neck, burrowing beneath my hair. I could feel her racing heartbeat begin to slow down as I gently stroked her head.

She was the cutest thing I'd ever seen. How bad could a piglet be?

"No problem, guys," I said. "You won't even notice she's here."

Chapter 2

THE CASE FOR KEEPING HAMLET

I told myself I wouldn't think about what Coach said at practice, but her words stung then, and they hurt now, even a week later when I was back at school.

The only one holding you back is you.

But it's not me! Or, at least, anything I can control. It's not like being outrageously tall was part of my grand plan or anything. All I've ever wanted was to be a great gymnast, not some freakish giant.

I slammed my locker shut, and a face appeared behind it.

"Welcome back to school!" he said.

"*Sully!* You scared me!" I exclaimed, nearly dropping my math book. Sully lived two townhouses down from me—just past Fernanda and Carlos's place—and we'd been close friends for as long as I could remember. He was one of the few kids on my block that went to HMS.

"Ahhhh," he said, studying me. "You're doing that thing."

"What thing?"

"You know. *The wrinkled forehead thing.* When you're thinking too hard about something."

I felt my cheeks burn hot. I wasn't about to blab to Sully about my gymnastics problems. But I *did* have something to tell him. It seemed like everyone—except my family, of course—had left town this year for Thanksgiving break, and I'd been waiting anxiously to introduce Hamlet to my friends.

"Do you have basketball practice today?" I asked, and Sully nodded. "Okay. Meet at the Three Stoops after. Loop the bike chain, so everyone knows, okay?"

The Three Stoops got its name back in fifth grade when Carlos and Fernanda moved in next door to me, and we all became friends because our three town-houses in a row—Sully, me, and the twins—all had identical redbrick steps.

Sully and I were two of the only people we knew who didn't have cell phones. Years ago, when we first started our regular meetings on the stoop, we started a secret way of communicating to our group: looping an old, rusty pink bike chain that once belonged to Sully's older sister around the front gate. Now whenever we see it, we spread the word to our friends on the block that someone has called a meeting.

"A meeting? Why?" Sully squinted his eyes as if he was trying to read my thoughts. I grinned. I wasn't about to give this secret away. I wanted to see his face when he met Hamlet for the first time.

"I have a surprise."

"What is it?"

"It won't be a surprise if I tell you!"

Sully threw me one of his classic goofy grins as he slowly backed away toward the Science lab. "You got it!" he said, pretending to shoot a ball into a basket, before slipping into the classroom.

The school day dragged on like it always does during the holiday season, when all you want is a magical snowstorm to sweep through so you can stay home, drink hot chocolate with peppermint sticks, and watch all your favorite Christmas movies. I sat alone on the bus home and squeezed my eyes shut, visualizing the Level 5 balance beam routine, pretending I was *step, step, stepping* down the length of it, until finally the bus pulled to a stop on my street.

The bus doors squeaked open, and a cool beginning-of-winter breeze swept across my open neck as I hopped off. The air this time of year always feels crisp against the skin, with a sharpness that makes you wide-eyed and alert. Soon the snow would be rolling in, and the brisk winds would blow for months on end.

I turned up the street and fiddled with the zipper of my puffy winter jacket, the bluish-purple one that Sarah wore all last year. I looked like a giant blueberry wearing it and there was a hole in one pocket, but it wasn't like Mom was going to buy me a new coat when this one fit me just fine.

Fallen, dried leaves gathered on the steps to our house, and a breeze sent them spinning. I call it a "house" but it's not a real one, not in the normal way that you see in movies, with a big grassy lawn and drive-way. Houses in this part of the city are long and thin, like matchbooks stacked right alongside one another, with two or three levels to each one. We all have tiny backyards and shared walls and fences, which was why Dad was always saying, "Quiet down, kids! There are humans around!" His catchphrases drove my sisters and me bonkos, but we also knew what my dad knew:

too much noise, and we'd be dealing with Mrs. Taglioni next door. *Ugh.*

Inside the house, Hamlet was practically screeching until I leaned over the old plastic baby gate we'd put across the nook and picked her up. Her heartbeat raced faster than mine at gymnastics practice! She wriggled for a moment before her muscles relaxed, until finally she rooted her snout right into my warm scarf. It tickled, sending me into hysterical laughter. It seemed like Hamlet knew just how to make me feel better.

I stroked my palm across the soft hairs along her back and whispered, "I know you don't like being left alone, but sometimes we just have things to do." Hamlet's ears twitched, listening. "And you're going to have to keep it down with all your squealing, or Mrs. Taglioni will come pound on our door. Trust me, neither of us want to deal with her! Okay, ready for a walk?"

I reached for her leash. Well, technically it was Sugar's old ratty leash. It was another thing Hamlet and I had in common: hand-me-downs.

We slipped out the back door. But as the screen door slammed behind me, I tripped over Amelia's bicycle, let go of Hamlet's leash, and totally wiped out on the patio. Hamlet danced across the yard as I got to my feet, kicking my little sister's bike tire. *Ugh!* She was going to get a mouthful next time I saw her!

"Ahhhhh, c'mon Hamlet," I said, reaching for her leash. But each time I got close to catching it, she galloped across the yard, until finally she scrambled up the porch steps and discovered an old potato chip bag— probably Amelia's—and nuzzled her snout right into it.

"Not a chance! Gotcha!" I snatched up her leash and tugged her back. "There's no way you're still hungry. You ate all the corn in your bowl! Now, let's go."

Hamlet squealed and oinked in protest, pulling and rooting her snout deeper into the bag until all I could see was her ears sticking out. I carried her out the back gate and down the little alleyway, past the garbage Dumpsters and recycling bins, until I was back on the main street outside my house.

I peeked down the block—no sign of Sully, the twins, or Lucy yet, and the bike chain wasn't looped on Sully's front gate. Hamlet was so happy to be outside, she sniffed at the air with her tongue half-sticking out of her mouth.

"Okay, okay," I said, finally giving in to her squirming, and set her down on the sidewalk. I glanced around nervously; there were only one or two taxicabs driving down the street, and no one seemed to be paying attention to the pig. "But don't tell Mom and Dad. I'd be in so much trouble if they knew I was walking you down the block!"

A shiver passed over her body, but she pranced down the sidewalk, her hooves going *clip clop* against the cement. It made me laugh. She was more graceful than I'd been lately in my floor routines. Happier, too.

As we walked up and down the block, a smile crept across my face. Lucy, my best friend from my gymnastics team, was going to FREAK. OUT. She lived around the corner from us, but she'd been at her grandmother's house all weekend for Thanksgiving and was one of my friends who went to private school during the week, so I hadn't seen her in days.

She spotted me first, calling out, "Hey, Josie!" from down the street. Then, "Wait—what is that?!" She ran up to us and dropped to her knees. "A piglet! *How do you have a pig?!* Awwwwww, it's *soooooooo* cute! I can't believe this!"

Hamlet jumped into her lap and licked her face, making Lucy giggle. "I'll explain everything at the Three Stoops meeting!" I told her, giving the piglet's leash a gentle tug. "Bike chain's not up yet—want to walk her for a bit and loop back?"

"Sure!" Lucy said.

Since I was saving the piglet details for the group, our conversation shifted to gymnastics. It was usually my favorite thing to talk about, but lately I found myself wanting to avoid it.

"Have you . . . thought about what Coach told you?" Lucy asked, quickening her pace to keep up with my long stride. I felt my face flush, even though it was like forty degrees outside. Lucy was as best as best friends could get. She could read me like a book.

But still, I wasn't ready to talk about it.

"Um—what?" I mumbled, watching the streetlight turn from yellow to red. We both came to a stop at the intersection. I began to hum "Jingle Bell Rock," hoping she'd drop the whole conversation.

"Oh, c'mon, Josie." Her dark hair was flat ironed today, and she smoothed down her part with a palm. "The back tuck thing? You can't get frustrated. Then you'll never nail it." She smiled easily. "Mind over matter, you know?"

Lucy was quoting Coach. Coach always said that.

I promised myself I wouldn't cry about it, so I fought back the tears.

I wasn't going to break that promise. No way.

"Yeah. I know," I said.

Lucy probably heard the quiver in my voice, but she didn't push the issue. We walked in silence for the next block. I lowered my eyes to the sidewalk, avoiding the cracks in the cement.

Hamlet trotted alongside us. Another breeze swept through, making her shiver. "Oh, Hamlet! Here, I'll warm you up," I said, lifting the piglet into my arms.

We walked past the library, around the big church on the corner, and down the block. By the time we circled back to the Three Stoops, Sully, Carlos, and Fernanda were waiting on the cement steps.

Carlos was in the middle of a story—he was always talking about *something*!—but stopped short when he saw us. "Josie!" he exclaimed. "What in the WHAT?!"

They all jumped to their feet and suddenly everyone was talking at once. Hamlet galloped right up to the Three Stoops like she was one of the gang, nestling into Fernanda's polka dot coat, while the questions fired my way, one right after another.

"Her name is Hamlet," I told my friends. "She's a runt. Tom saved her from his girlfriend's farm."

"She's sooooo little," cooed Fernanda.

I nodded. "She's only a few weeks old, but boy, does she have some appetite! I feel like I'm constantly feeding her."

"What does she eat?" asked Carlos.

"Mostly milk right now. I'm using one of Amelia's baby doll bottles! And we picked up some dry pellet food for her over the weekend, but since she's so young, I have to soak it with milk until it's super mushy."

"Awwww, she's sure SOME PIG!" said Lucy. She was quoting *Charlotte's Web*, one of our favorite books. I grinned. Being with Lucy was always so carefree and easy. I felt lucky that she was on my gymnastics team, but life would be even better if we went to the same school.

But as Lucy moved to stand next to me, the smile vanished from my face. My little sister, Amelia, was right—I was practically a whole foot taller than Lucy now, and standing side by side in front of all our friends made my height seem weirdly obvious. I hunched my shoulders and sat down on the stoop next to Carlos.

"I heard pigs are really smart," said Carlos. "Oh, hey, cool! Her tail uncurls when you scratch her back, right on her spots."

Sully spun his baseball cap around. "I can't believe

your parents are letting you keep a pig."

"Ugh, they're not. . . . That's also why I called a meeting. I need your help."

"Help for what?" asked Fernanda. "Ack—Hamlet! She's getting tangled in my hair!"

Her brother laughed, reaching for the piglet's collar and pulling her back. "Ohhhh, we've got a slobbery one here, guys."

I smiled, remembering the moment I got to hold Hamlet for the first time, and how she couldn't stop licking my hands, and how all I wanted to do was stare at her adorable snout and into her big brown eyes.

"I promised my parents that I'd find Hamlet a home by New Year's Day, but I want to keep her," I explained. "So I have about a month to convince them why that's a good idea."

"Hmmm." Fernanda tapped her chin.

"Can I take a picture of her?" Lucy asked. "My gran won't believe this when I tell her!"

Hamlet's eyes were half-closed and her tongue flopped out of her mouth a little, which reminded me of Sugar when she sunbathes too long. But Hamlet wasn't hot—it was much too cold out for that. She was just *happy*.

"Sure."

Lucy pulled her cell phone out of her back pocket and snapped a picture of Hamlet. The great thing about Lucy is that she did it casually and quickly instead of rubbing it in my face that I didn't have a phone.

It's not like we were poor or anything. The Shilling household was just *full*. My parents carefully considered every purchase during their weekly budget meeting in the living room. "To protect our future," they told us. I believed them. It's just how things were. If I wanted something badly enough, I saved my allowance money for it.

"So, you guys," I continued, "I need to open up a new Case File."

Sully's eyes widened, the way they always do when a new case is opened. He wants to be a police detective when he grows up, and he's always investigating all sorts of things in the neighborhood.

"Wait! Wait!" he said, reaching into his backpack. He retrieved a little spiral notebook with a pencil tied to the wire with a rubber band, flipping to a new lined page. At the top, he carefully wrote out: "THE CASE FOR KEEPING HAMLET."

"Perfect." I grinned. With all five of us thinking on

this, it would be a piece of cake to convince my parents why Hamlet should be our new pet.

"Wait a sec," said Carlos, reaching for the colored pencil tucked behind his ear. He took the notebook from Sully, drew a quick sketch of a pig at the top of the page, and handed the notebook back.

"Hey, that's really good," I said. Carlos had been into drawing for as long as I'd known him, but this year he was taking classes at the local Community Center, the same place where my mom worked.

"Reason number one," declared Lucy, placing a hand over her heart. "Because Hamlet is officially the Most Adorable Piglet in the World."

Fernanda pushed a curl back from her eyes. "I'm not sure that will convince Josie's dad," she said thoughtfully. "He's not really an animal person."

I held back a laugh, remembering that one time Fernanda was over for dinner and Dad spilled pasta onto his work shoes and Sugar squeezed underneath the table and starting licking the leather. He had been *so* grossed out!

"Then I have reason number two!" Lucy countered, pointing to Sully's pencil. He pressed it to the notepad, waiting for her idea. "Maybe your dad doesn't like

Sugar, but your mom sure does! What if Sugar's lonely and needs a furry friend?"

Our golden retriever was old, and she pretty much napped all day long. I wasn't sure how lonely she was. But it was true that Mom really liked Sugar, so maybe it was a good strategy.

"Hamlet's not really furry," countered Fernanda.

"More like a *hairy* friend," suggested Carlos. Sully made a note of it in the Case File.

"Let's keep thinking," I said. "I've gotta run—I have social studies homework."

"Don't forget about the quiz tomorrow!" Fernanda said, giving me two thumbs-up. She was one of the best students in our class. I nodded.

Carlos reached for the Case File again, showing Sully about the new techniques he was learning in calligraphy by writing "PIG PIG PIG" over and over again at the top of the page. Sully nodded, and I could tell he was still on the case, busy thinking through more reasons Hamlet should stay on our block. Good—I needed all my friends' ideas!

"Josie, I'm coming with you," Lucy said, skipping to my side. Since she lived past my house and around the corner, it was an unofficial tradition that she walked me to my door after Three Stoops meetings. "See you guys later!"

As we walked down the block, Hamlet tried to bite at the long leather leash and danced on her hooves. She was as playful as a puppy! When we got to my door, I unzipped my coat pocket, slipping my hand inside the down fabric, searching for the cool metal of the front door key.

Suddenly, my breath caught in my throat.

I'd lost my house key.

Chapter 3

UNDER LOCK AND KEY

I checked my pocket again. Usually it wouldn't be a big deal to get locked out. It's not like it's the first time this has happened or anything. But what *was* a big deal was that I lost the spare key, and it was the only spare key we had. The temperature was dropping and Hamlet trembled from the cold, and since Lucy had to leave soon to be with her family, it's not like I could just take a pig to her place and stay there without supervision.

But the *biggest reason* was that I couldn't get in trouble with my parents.

Not now with my gymnastics meet coming up and Hamlet's life in my hands. If I couldn't keep track of a house key, they'd never trust me with a pet pig!

"Lucy," I said, my voice shaking.

My best friend's jaw dropped at my tone. "What is it?"

"My key! It's not in my pocket . . ."

"Oh. Well, check the other one?"

"But I always use the right one."

I slid my hand into my left coat pocket just to be sure. It was empty except for loose coins and a hair tie. I felt my heartbeat skyrocket as I patted down my jeans pockets, too. No sign of the house key.

"Just knock on the door! You live with like a million people," said Lucy casually. She scooped Hamlet up into her arms, and the piglet snuggled against her warm coat. "Oh, Hammie's cold! I'll warm you up, Hammie."

"No one's home. . . ." I shook my head. "Ellen's at band practice, Amelia's at Lou's house, Mom's working her shift at the Community Center, Sarah had a PSAT session with friends, and Dad's getting an oil change for the van. . . ."

Lucy rubbed noses with Hamlet and giggled. "What about Tom?" she said, still unfazed.

"Back at school."

Lucy was an only child, so she didn't always understand how things worked in the Shilling family. She lived in calm, and we lived in chaos. There are days when you never have a moment alone, and then there are days like today, when there's no one around when you need someone.

I peeked down the block, and from my angle I could see the Three Stoops had already disbanded—not one of our friends was in sight.

"Oh, Lucy . . ." I said, trying not to cry. "I'm not supposed to take Hamlet out of the backyard. My parents will know that I left the house with her, and I didn't ask for permission. The only way they'll let me keep her is if I show them how responsible I am—"

"Don't cry, don't cry!" Lucy's eyebrows lifted. "Here, hold Hammie. She'll make you feel better while we talk this out."

She transferred the little piglet into my arms. I stroked her ears back, trying to think. Where was that key? Hamlet lifted her snout into the air, catching a scent that triggered a series of oinks.

"She's the cutest!" laughed Lucy.

SLAM!

I felt the color drain from my face. I knew that jolting sound by heart—I'd heard it countless times over the years. I spun around, faking my most cheerful, not-doing-anything-wrong face.

Mrs. Taglioni stood on her front stoop. It was like a permanent scowl was tattooed on her face. Sure, she was nice enough to the grown-ups on the block, but she couldn't stand us kids. She lived alone with her old, giant cat, Tootsie, and, legend had it, two sugar gliders, even though I've never seen them. But Sarah told me that her Wi-Fi password was *sugar glider*, so the rumors had to be true. According to Sarah, sugar gliders look like flying squirrels, but they're actually related to kangaroos. I can't vouch for that because I've never seen one before.

"Ahhh—you two. Making noise on the street again. How about leaving an old woman with some peace and quiet?" Mrs. Taglioni rattled her doorknob to ensure her house was locked.

"Hi, Mrs. Taglioni," we said in unison.

She patted her pulled-back dark hair, which sort of resembled a bird's nest, and eyed us suspiciously. Hamlet wouldn't stop writhing out of my grasp, and I couldn't risk her squealing at the top of her piglet lungs, so I placed her on the stoop right behind the dead potted plant. Mrs. Taglioni might like exotic creatures like sugar gliders, but there was no way she would like a farm pig living next door, especially if it made more noise than us Shilling kids.

I tried to spin around before Mrs. Taglioni laid eyes on her, but it was too late.

"What. Is. That. *Creature?*"

"Hamlet!" I said brightly, not answering her question directly, but answering it at the same time. Sometimes avoiding things was the best way to keep Mrs. Taglioni happy—I learned that from Tom. I wrapped my scarf around Hamlet's bare belly, so she was just a little head peeking out from the fabric.

"Hamlet," Mrs. Taglioni repeated, adjusting her thick spectacles on her nose. She stood maybe ten feet away from us, but her stare was so penetrating, it felt like *five* feet. I tried to block Hamlet with my body, and hoped Mrs. Taglioni's eyeglass lenses were dirty. "You got a puppy?"

"We're pet sitting for a while," I said, which wasn't really an answer either.

"Well. It better not bark during *Jeopardy!*" Mrs. Taglioni clutched the railing as she moved down her stoop steps. Once she was out of earshot, I spun around and met Lucy's wide eyes.

"Phew," Lucy whispered.

"Close one!" I agreed, exhaling loudly. "Okay. The

key . . . the key . . . I've got to find it. . . ."

"Retrace your steps," Lucy said. "That's what I always do when I lose something. It's gotta be around here *somewhere*, right? Keys don't just run away. I have a few minutes before I have to leave—I'll help you look. Now. Pretend you're leaving the house, just like before. . . ."

"Good idea." I picked up Hamlet and held her close. "Okay—first, I got Hamlet's leash, and we went out through the backyard. . . ."

Lucy nodded. "Okay, let's check the back!"

We slipped into the alley behind our house, carefully searching the ground all along the fence until we got to the gate to our little backyard. It was only a thirty-second walk, but carrying a squirming piglet and with your parents due home soon, it sure felt like twenty minutes!

Hamlet was getting strong, too. Even in the four days we'd had her it already seemed like she had gained a few pounds. She wiggled and wriggled in my arms until finally, once Lucy opened up the gate, I set her down in our yard.

We searched and searched and searched for the missing house key. It wasn't on the stone patio, or underneath Amelia's bike, which was still lying on its side where I'd tripped over it, or alongside Dad's grill.

"Knock on the back door?" Lucy suggested. "Maybe someone came home through the front."

"No way. I have to find the key first, or I'll be in so much trouble." As panic overwhelmed my senses, a burning sensation rose from my stomach. What if I lost it on the sidewalk? It was one thing to lose a key in the backyard, but quite another to lose it on the city streets. Most of the time our neighborhood was pretty safe, but my parents would still be mad all the same.

And maybe . . . I felt my heart thump wildly in my chest.

I could get grounded.

If that happened, I wouldn't be allowed to compete in the upcoming meet.

My throat went dry.

Gymnastics meant everything to me. It was the one thing I had that was really mine. Without it, I was doomed!

Hamlet's loud oink reached my ears. Mom and Dad said I had to be responsible to keep her—that they trusted me. If I got grounded for being careless and losing the house key, maybe they'd send her away to a bacon farm before the New Year's Day deadline.

Hamlet would be doomed, too.

And it would be my fault.

"Uh . . . Josie?" Lucy said. She reached for Hamlet's leash and tugged the little pig my way. "Hamlet might've gotten into your mom's garden. . . ."

I looked up. Hamlet was covered in garden soil, from ears to hooves to curlicue tail. I groaned and took the leash from Lucy's hand just as her phone buzzed. She checked the text message.

"It's my mom—I gotta go! I'm sorry! They're waiting on me for dinner." Her eyebrows pinched together. "You'll be okay with the key and . . . everything?"

I nodded, but only because I couldn't find the strength to use words. Inside, I was flipping out. Not only was the house key missing, now Hamlet was a muddy mess, and somehow I needed to find the key *and* clean her up before my family got home.

"Maybe you should come over," Lucy said. She glanced at Hamlet and bit her lip, and I knew what she was thinking—that there was no way a muddy pig was going to be allowed in her house.

"I can't leave Hamlet here—like this and in the cold," I told her. She sighed in agreement.

"If you don't find the key in ten minutes, just come

over, okay?" she told me. "Even if you have to bring Hammie with you. We'll figure something out. Everything will be all right . . . Okay?" Lucy gave me a big squeeze. "See you in ten minutes—or tomorrow at practice!"

"Yep," I said, forcing a smile as she skipped out the back gate.

Okay. I was on my own to figure this out. I glanced at the unwound hose, flopped across the stone patio. It was much too cold out to rinse a little piglet outside. Hamlet needed a warm bath. But to make that happen, I needed to get inside.

Hamlet trotted alongside of me, muddy as could be. It looked like her little pink body had been dipped in milk chocolate. I pressed my shoulders back and lifted my chin, as if I was about to begin a gymnastics routine.

I was going to figure my way out of this mess. I *had* to.

Hamlet rooted her snout into the potato chip bag on the patio, grunting and squeezing until her whole head was wedged inside, leaving just her gray-spotted behind and pink tail sticking out.

"Hamlet! What is it *with* you and that darn potato chip bag? Ughhhhh, Millie really needs to learn to clean up after herself." I gripped my hands around Hamlet's little belly and pulled the bag off her head.

Clink!

Something silver fell on the patio.

A memory sparked, and my eyes lit up. I had tripped over Amelia's bike! The key must've fallen out then, and somehow Hamlet had rooted it into the bag. I couldn't believe it. Ellen said pigs were smart—even smarter than dogs. Maybe Hamlet had been trying to warn me earlier that my key had fallen on the ground. I picked up the key, the cool metal tingling my palm.

"You saved the day!" I cheered, scratching behind Hamlet's ears. "Best piggy in the world!"

Now all I had to do was give Hamlet a bath before anyone got home. We unlocked the back door and slipped inside before anyone saw us.

Except for Sarah.

She stood in the hallway, mouth half open and a spoonful of yogurt in her hand. The name "ELLEN" was handwritten on the side of the yogurt cup in scribbled black ink. Normally I would've scolded Sarah for stealing it from the fridge, but right now I couldn't risk annoying her.

Sarah's gaze lowered to the doormat, where Hamlet

was rubbing her dirty hooves into the rubber. An amused smirk spread across her face.

"Dad's upstairs," she warned me. "A little advice? Van had a leaking oil pan. I'd keep the filthy farm animal away from him." Her nose wrinkled. "Ugh, and the pig reeks."

I swallowed hard. She didn't need to remind me. But I wouldn't be able to reach the bathroom undetected without Sarah's help . . . and getting my fifteen-year-old sister to help me with *anything* seemed downright impossible these days.

"You've got to distract him," I begged. "Please! I'll give Hamlet a quick bath before dinnertime. No one has to notice."

Sarah shook her head. "No can do, Shortcake," she said. "This is your responsibility, not mine. I'm busy studying for the PSAT." Sarah plopped the spoon back into her yogurt cup and rounded the hall corner into the kitchen.

I sighed and looked toward the stairwell. The coast was clear—for now. I picked Hamlet up and held her tightly in my arms.

It was go time!

Chapter 4

THE DOCTOR IS IN

I tiptoed up the stairs as quietly as possible. I didn't realize I was holding my breath until my lungs began to ache. The bathroom was right around the corner. I exhaled—we were almost there!

Then the top step creaked beneath my boot.

No!

"Sarah?" Dad called out. My parents' bedroom door was cracked ajar. I'd have to breeze by to make it to the bathroom. I rewrapped my scarf around Hamlet's body, shielding her just like before, when Mrs. Taglioni was on her stoop.

"Sarah?"

I bit my lip. If I ignored him, he might come into the

hallway. "No, Dad, it's Josie," I said, tiptoeing across the wood floor.

"Oh. Okay," Dad said, his voice carrying through the open door. "I thought Sarah needed help with her practice test. I'll be down in a bit. I'm just resting until dinnertime."

He *did* sound exhausted. "Sure, Dad. I'll be quiet." I slipped past the doorway, the piglet secretly in my arms.

I set the pig down on the bathroom floor and twisted the faucet knobs until warm water began to fill the bathtub. It turned out that Hamlet not only loved getting muddy, she loved getting clean. She burrowed her face in the bubbles and sneezed them off her snout. I scrubbed behind her twitchy ears and rubbed the dirt from the fine hairs across her back. Carlos was right— whenever you scratched right over her spots, her little curly tail would relax and then spring up like a coil again.

Hamlet gave me a big lick across the cheek, making me laugh. Muddy or clean, she was the best pig in the world.

A sinking feeling crept over me as I dried her off with a towel. Dad said I shouldn't get attached. Maybe he was right, that a tiny city house wasn't a good place to raise a pig. But still, if she stayed with us, she would be safe and loved.

Didn't that make it the best kind of house?

Hamlet's eyes closed, and she began to fall asleep in her little towel burrito. Soft snores reached my ears.

I just *had* to convince my parents that we should keep her.

The bathroom door burst open. "Lou's mom is in the living room!" said Amelia, sliding across the tiles in her socks. "Whoa . . . whoa . . . WHOA!" She caught herself on the sink just in time.

"Millie!" I scolded, lifting the piglet into the safety of my arms. "You could've clobbered Hamlet! And broken your arm—or *my* arm!"

"Sor-*ry*!"

My mind raced. Lou was Amelia's best friend, and his mom was a veterinarian who operated an animal clinic a few blocks away. What was she doing in *our* living room?

"She's waiting for you downstairs," Amelia said.

"Why?"

"She called Mom this afternoon. Something about Hamlet, I dunno?"

The hair on the back of my neck tingled. What if Dr.

Stern found something wrong with Hamlet? Or—*even worse*—took her away from us?

I narrowed my eyes. "You and Lou just *had* to blab about the pig, didn't you? Two big mouths." My sister's cheeks turned a bright shade of pink, but she didn't argue. "We'll continue this later," I said, getting to my feet. Hamlet's heart was racing, too, so I gently stroked her back, letting her know that everything would be okay. As I left Amelia in the bathroom, I called out behind me, "*And go move your bike off the patio already and stop littering!*" and stomped downstairs, totally forgetting that Dad was resting in my parents' bedroom.

Dr. Stern sat on our vintage sofa in the living room. When she saw me, she set her cup of coffee on the side table. "Hiya, Josie," she said. "So this must be Hamlet!"

I paused, unsure of what to say. I'd always liked Dr. Stern. She had short, silver-black hair, kind dark eyes, and a peaceful energy that just wasn't in the Shilling family genes. I smiled back, but it felt impossible to squelch the fear brewing inside me.

"Dr. Stern is just taking a quick look at Hamlet," Mom explained, as if she could sense my anxiety.

The vet motioned at the piglet. "Why don't you set her down here?"

I didn't move. Hamlet wasn't allowed on the living room carpet. I saw Mom's gaze shift toward the stairway and then back at me. She gave me a wink and a nod.

I gently placed the piglet on the carpet. Dr. Stern leaned over and stroked Hamlet's back. The pig seemed to like her immediately because she didn't wiggle away. I sat down next to Hamlet, and as I watched her be examined, I realized just how much Hamlet had really plumped up over the last few days.

Dr. Stern put a stethoscope against the piglet's belly. "She's got a strong heartbeat," she commented. "Want to hear it?"

"Sure!"

She showed me how to wear the headset and slide the chest piece across Hamlet's skin until it was in just the right place. The piglet's heartbeat made a gentle *thump thump* sound in my ears.

"What're you checking her for?" I asked Dr. Stern, handing her back the stethoscope.

"Well." She ruffled through the medical bag. "Hamlet is from a region with a high pseudorabies status, so I thought it best to do a quick blood test."

I drew in a deep breath. "Does that mean she's sick?"

She smiled easily. "Don't worry. Hamlet appears to

be in great health. It's just a precaution. We should contact another veterinarian about vaccinations, deworming treatments, and filing her hooves though. Now." She pulled measuring tape from her bag and wrapped it around the pig's belly and neck, writing measurements down in a small notebook.

I figured I should ask the big question that was weighing on my heart. I knew that Hamlet needed a forever home . . . but I was hoping that would be right here, in our house. Somewhere she'd be safe and loved.

"Are you going to take her away from us?"

Dr. Stern exchanged a look with my mother. "Not right now," she assured me. Hamlet let out a loud *oink*, like she was happy to hear that she was staying for a while longer, too. I ran my palm along the length of her hairy back, and she oinked again, making Dr. Stern laugh. "She sure seems to like you."

"Thanks." I grinned. *Reason number three for the Case for Keeping Hamlet!* "I like her a lot, too."

There was a loud *thump!* on the back door. Amelia and Lou were throwing a tennis ball against the house again. I wrinkled my nose. My sister should be moving her bike and raking leaves off the back patio steps. If they kept up that ruckus, Dad would come downstairs to investigate, and I didn't want him to get mad about Hamlet being off her leash in the living room.

"Now." Dr. Stern clapped her hands together. "Why don't you show me—what do you call it? Hamlet's Cave?"

Mom beamed at me. "That's a great idea!"

"Okay."

Hamlet trotted at my heels as I gave Dr. Stern the tour of her little spot beneath the stairs. I told the veterinarian about how the piglet learned how to use a litter box after just a few days' time, and what brand of cedar chips I used in her Cave, and how her stomach never seemed full, no matter how much food I fed her.

Dr. Stern laughed. "Pigs do like to eat. But be careful not to overfeed her, because that's bad for her health."

I nodded. "Ellen told me that pigs are super smart," I said. "Is that true?"

"Yes. Some studies found that pigs can learn tricks, like using a video game joystick, standing on their hind legs, and even bowing."

"Hamlet, *bowing*?" I laughed, imagining such a sight. "That'd be something!"

"Did you know that pigs can learn something so quickly, that they can master it on the first try?"

I felt nerves jolt in my stomach all over again, thinking about the new gymnastics skills I was trying to learn. It was taking me forever to nail them down. It'd be pretty amazing to master a new routine after attempting it just once.

"Well, Hamlet did pretty good with litter box training, so I believe it."

Loud snores reached our ears. Dr. Stern glanced over at Sugar, who was lying in front of the heating vent. "How is Hamlet getting along with the dog?"

"Pretty well, actually," said Mom.

"Mostly they just ignore each other," I added, but then remembered reason number two for the Case for Keeping Hamlet. "But I think Sugar really, *really* likes the company."

"Oh, you do, honey?" Mom glanced at the dog thoughtfully. "That's nice to hear."

Dr. Stern nodded. "Pigs are social animals, so it's good to let her spend time with other animals and people."

"Hear that, Mom? Hamlet needs more free time in the house."

"Hmm, that's certainly something to think about, isn't it." Mom didn't smile back, but her tone was light, so it felt like a promise of some kind.

"Well," Dr. Stern said, lifting her medical bag over her shoulder. "Hamlet seems to be doing very well, given the circumstances. But keep looking for a permanent home for her, okay, Josie? The city isn't the best place for a pig."

"Yep! I'm working on it," I assured her, walking the veterinarian to the front door. "And thanks for giving Hamlet an exam."

I was already memorizing new reasons for the Case File:

Reason #4—The Pig Is Very Healthy

Reason #5—She Is Attached to Josie

Reason #6—She Is Very Smart and Can Learn Tricks

I started to turn the doorknob but stopped. There was one more question I wanted to ask Dr. Stern before she left.

I swallowed hard. *Be brave,* I told myself. *Be confident like Tom.*

"Dr. Stern?"

She looped a wool scarf around her neck. "Yes, Josie?"

"You know that measuring tape in your bag? Do you—" I cleared my throat. I had to know if it was all in my mind, or if it was real. "Do you think you could measure how tall I am?"

Chapter 5

PEP TALK TIME

Whenever I needed advice, I called Tom.

Of course it took me four times to actually *reach* my brother in his dorm room, but finally he called me back, right after I played with Hamlet in the backyard and before Dad drove me to gymnastics practice.

"What's up, JoJo?" Tom said when I picked up the phone. "Happy December!"

"Um. Happy December."

So far, December wasn't feeling happy at all. I had thirty-one days left to convince my parents that I should keep Hamlet as a pet, and so far it didn't seem to be working. Dad never seemed to notice how often I cleaned her Cave, and that I'd bought air fresheners for the downstairs hallway so it would always smell nice and fresh in the house. Hamlet never squealed from being hungry because I was consistent with feeding her, three times a day, and ensured she always had fresh, clean water.

And then there was gymnastics. My stomach had felt sour and twisted all day, just thinking about the skills I was falling short on. But Tom had this way of always staying positive no matter what was going on in his life. I'd seen him grinning ear to ear after playing his best on the football field, and after his worst games too, when none of the plays seemed to go the way he'd hoped.

"I, um, need your help," I said, twisting the cord of the kitchen phone around my finger.

"About Hamlet?" Tom's cheerful tone deflated. "Sorry, sis, but I tried everything I could, and football—"

"Not about Hamlet," I cut in, although I still hadn't solved the Case for Keeping Hamlet, so that was technically a problem, too. I glanced around the corner, just to be sure that Sarah was still upstairs studying and that my dad wasn't listening in on our conversation. I lowered my voice. "It's about *gymnastics*."

"Ahhhh. Sports talk. My specialty!" The mouthpiece of the phone buzzed static, like Tom was pressing the phone more closely to his ear. "Go for it."

"Well." I cleared my throat, not quite sure how to

express how I was feeling in words. But I was going to give it a shot. If anyone could help me, it'd be Tom. "So, you know how I moved up to Level Five this year? We've been learning all these new routines. There's a big meet in a few weeks, right before Christmas. Maybe Mom told you about it? Anyways. I'm—I'm having trouble with a few things."

"What's the trouble?"

I exhaled. Here it goes. "I'm too tall to do the skills."

There was a long pause. "Josie," Tom said, his tone serious. "You're telling me it's *physically impossible* for you to do the new routines?"

I could almost see Tom's eyebrows lifting in disbelief. I squeezed my eyes shut, trying to block out his face in my mind. That's why phone calls were easier sometimes. I felt myself close down inside at the sight of a single disappointed look. I'd learned that the hard way from my parents, teachers, and coaches over the years. I couldn't feel that way toward my brother, not now, when I needed his help the most.

"Yes. I mean, no." I sighed again. "I'm not sure. It's just . . . things are so much different this season. A lot harder! I'm *so much* taller than last year. I know that for a fact because Dr. Stern measured me the other day—"

"A vet measured your height?"

"Yeah . . . well, she was here checking Hamlet, and I figured . . . anyways, you're missing the point. Hey, Tom! Stop laughing! It's not funny."

"Okay, okay!"

"I need you serious right now."

"Totally serious. Keep going."

I drew in another deep breath. *"Like I was saying . . . I'm so much taller than the other girls on my team now. And—and it's just not fair."*

"Ah. So there we have it."

"You should see Lucy's long haul kip on the uneven bars. She's amazing!" I continued. "Her flyaway dismount gives me goose bumps. And Jenna nails her back walkover on the balance beam every time, and I keep falling off, no matter how hard I concentrate. I just can't control it right anymore, especially when I work on my form. And don't get me started on my back handspring step out. It's like—it's like my *angles* are all different. Even things that used to be easy are really hard now." I squeezed my eyes shut, thinking of my hands catching the bar and my wobbly turns on the balance beam.

"JoJo." Tom's voice was calm. "Lemme tell you a story, okay? When the college football scouts came to my high school games senior year, you know what I was thinking about? Playing my best. If I was out there on the field, worrying about who was bigger and better than me, you know where I'd be right now? Not here, playing for a championship team, I guarantee you that. You just can't worry about the other guys—er, girls. It's gotta be about *you* in the game, or what's the point? It's not worth your time and energy if your heart's not in it for the right reasons. There's always gonna be someone better. *Always.* That's part of life, you know? Let the good ones inspire you to be the best *you* that you can be and work hard to make it happen."

I bit my lip. He sounded like Coach. I knew that being jealous of the other girls wasn't helping anything. But still, Tom's advice didn't solve my height problem either.

Tom continued, as if he was reading my mind. "I know you think we're these giant people, JoJo, but we're really not. You should see some of the guys on my team. This one dude, Luke, is nearly seven feet tall. Seriously! I'm actually one of the shorter guys. But I'm fast, and I use that to my advantage. We've all got something to bring to the team. So you know what? Being a tall gymnast has gotta have a perk to it, kinda like being speedy in football. You're only seeing what the other girls are good at and what you're having trouble with. .... But what skills can you do well that maybe the others find challenging?"

I rolled my shoulders back, considering. "I'm not sure."

"JOSIE, I'LL BE OUT FRONT!"

I glanced over my shoulder, following the sound of Dad's voice. "Tom, gotta run. Dad's driving me to practice now—BE RIGHT THERE!"

"*Dad's* driving you?"

"I know. Never happens. Something about prepping for a conference call later. He probably wants to use the gymnastics gym Wi-Fi." I untwisted the phone cord from my finger. "I'll think about what you said. And thanks."

"Anytime, sis. Go get 'em."

We hung up the phone, and I did a quick check on Hamlet, filling up her water bowl and pouring another cup of feed in her bowl. She was curled up, napping in her Cave. I gave her a gentle scratch behind the ears and kiss on the head.

"See you later, Hammie," I whispered. A horn honked loudly outside. Dad gets impatient when the van is double-parked on the street.

I slung my gymnastics bag over my shoulder, racing outside. Dad gave me a stressed smile from the driver's seat and turned the ignition. "Do we need to pick up Lucy?" he asked, and I shook my head. "All right, here we go!"

I stared out the window, watching the city streets whizz by us, lost in my thoughts. Maybe I'd been looking at my height the wrong way this entire time. Maybe I was good—or even *great*—at something without even realizing it, *because* I was tall. I tapped my foot against the floor mat.

I couldn't wait to get to gymnastics and find out.

Chapter 6

LET'S GET READY TO TUMBLE

After warm-up and conditioning, my team stood along-side the padded gymnasium floor. The gym smelled of sweat and chalk, and over by the uneven bars, the Level 6 team all hung from the lower bar as they lifted their legs up to the bar and back down, over and over again.

I stretched, waiting.

My lungs inflated.

The younger girls jumped on a tumble track in the background.

I exhaled.

Coach stood beside the iPod docking station, cueing the start to each of our routines. I closed my eyes, trying to block the sound of lockers slamming shut. When I opened them, I caught my reflection in the mirror along the length of the wall and was filled with horror. I was practically a head taller than some of the other girls. I licked the dryness from my lips, reminding myself of Tom's words earlier on the phone.

We've all got something to bring to the team.

"Maxie, you're up first," Coach said. "Remember, no loosey goosey arms in your jumps. Your arms need to move gracefully and with purpose! Ta-DA!"

Maxie nodded, adjusting her leotard while running to the center of the floor. As the music blared through the speakers, my pulse began to race as I anticipated my turn.

"Fast! Fast! Fast! Go!" Coach called out. "'Push off the hands! Hands! Hands! Hands! Elbows by your ears, Maxie!"

I think I zoned out for most of her routine, just trying to calm my nerves. It felt like the next time I blinked, Coach was staring at me, saying, "Josie, your turn."

"Are you spotting me?" I asked her. "I'm not sure I'm ready."

As soon as the words escaped my mouth, I wanted to swallow them back up. Coach didn't like it when we doubted ourselves. She said confidence was one of the best traits a gymnast can have.

Coach studied me for a moment. "Let's just do one more pass together in the lane before you go. I'll be right there." I breathed a sigh of relief. She motioned for Lucy to cut the music, and I moved to the corner of the floor mat, where the white perimeter lines connect in a right triangle. "Ready," Coach told me from her position in the middle of the floor.

Step, step, KNEE *UP*!

I hurdled into the roundoff, keeping my body low and long as I powered into the back handspring. As my feet reached the floor, I punched down and followed my hands up and back, feeling Coach's guiding arm grazing across my skin as I tucked my knees to my chest.

"Hug! Hug! RELEASE!"

Coach's words were loud in my ears, but it was too late. I was going too fast and I released my knees late—I over-rotated the back tuck. If it weren't for Coach's spotting, which brought me back to my feet, I probably would've landed straight on my back.

"Sorry," I said, catching my breath. I heard a snicker from the sidelines and looked up to see the Level 10 team stretching in front of the mirror. I wasn't sure if the girls were giggling at me or not, but in the moment, it sure felt like I was the target.

I felt my cheeks burn red. Coach clapped the older girls away like pesky pigeons. "Ladies, move to the vault until Coach Stephanie arrives," she said sternly before turning to me. "You can do this, Josie. Don't let your nerves get ahold of you."

I swallowed hard. That was easier said than done. "Yeah. Okay."

"Now back to the line."

I bounded to the corner of the floor mat, tightened my ponytail, and nodded at Coach.

My timing was better on the second pass, but not great. After my turn was over, Coach sent me to the back of the line to visualize my routines.

By the time I was up again, my nerves were electric. "Full floor routine now, Josie," Coach told me. "Focus, focus, focus!"

I found my place in the middle of the floor and drew in a deep breath. I couldn't have her spotting me forever, but still—I felt like I needed her there, just in case.

I pretended that with each breath I drew, the more confidence filled me up. I placed my arms in second position. My heart beat wildly in my chest, like a fish trying to break free from a line. I let out a long, slow breath and waited for the music to begin.

This was it—my time to shine.

In front of Coach.

In front of the whole team.

I glanced across the gymnasium, searching for a familiar face.

It was also my chance to show my dad that I was good at something—but not just that. I wanted him to see that I belonged here, competing with my teammates. I wanted Dad to know that gymnastics meant something to me, but not because I told him. Because he saw it with his very own eyes.

The song's opening notes floated across the gym. I stretched my arms high above my head, as if catching the music in my palms. Here we go. Stay tight. Reach high. I leapt into my first straddle jump, pointing my toes.

So far, so good. The dance choreography came easy today. It was the tumbling pass I needed to hit. I felt my eyes shift from my fingertips to the team, their eyes locked on my movements. Coach studied me hard, her knuckles raised to her chin.

The only one holding you back is you.

I ran three steps and punched into a tight front tuck, flipping forward. "Reach up! Release and STICK!" Coach shouted, and I unwound my body into the standing position, feet pounding the floor, giving me too much bounce.

"Snap—and stand up! UP, JOSIE!"

The music trilled on. My nerves were getting the best of me. I sashayed into a leap. The new tumbling skill was still another thirty seconds way, but my mind was already preparing for it. I hit each standing jump and arm movement with precision. I pointed my toes. Spun my full turn. Kept my chest and chin lifted high.

I can do this.

I pranced toward the corner of the floor and turned to face its center. Five seconds of music passed. Five seconds to catch my breath.

I didn't let myself think about Coach not being there ready to spot me. I only thought about what my body needed to do. I pumped my arms and ran, then lifted my left knee up, propelling myself into a strong round-off. As soon as my feet hit the floor, I stretched high and back, arms lifted, body tight.

I felt free. I felt FIERCE.

It wasn't my power that surprised me this time. It was my control.

The back handspring was surprisingly solid. I squeezed my muscles and kept long and lean until my feet hit the floor again. It was almost too easy. I could've stopped myself on the landing, but I was so strong that I just SKYROCKETED upward into the air, and without even thinking it through, I tucked my knees to my chest, feet rotating over my head, and threw myself backward into the tuck.

"Look, look, LOOK!"

I looked for the floor, squeezing my body tight. Once I saw the flash of gray, I released the grip on my knees. The landing was solid, and I kept tight as I lifted my arms above my head, sticking it.

I couldn't believe it.

I nailed it. I totally nailed it, for the first time by myself, *ever*.

The music ended with me stretching out into a big lunge, hands in front of my chest, fingers curled, my chin tilted back. The sound of cheering reached my ears. I looked over at the team. Coach had a huge grin on her face as she clapped along with the girls. Lucy was jumping up and down.

I smiled so big my cheeks hurt.

"Nicely done, Josie," Coach said, nodding in approval. She'd never said I'd nicely done anything before.

I raised my eyes to the bleachers, searching for my

dad. But he wasn't looking at me. He was typing on his laptop. He didn't even notice that the biggest moment of my life had just happened in this very room.

I walked over my team. "Whoa, Josie, that was ah-MAZING," Lucy whispered in my ear.

But I hardly heard her. My dad was here—and he hadn't even watched. I blinked back the tears and sat down on the floor, wrapping my arms around my knees while the other girls took their turns.

After practice, we sat in silence for most of the drive home. Dad's cell phone kept ringing over and over, but the van didn't have Bluetooth—of course—so he couldn't answer it. It just rang and rang. Even though I wanted to chuck it out the window, I didn't.

"Can I turn off the volume?" I asked Dad after the fourth call in five minutes.

Dad glanced my way. "Sure," he said, but his voice had a worried quality about it.

I turned toward the window. Even though it got dark super early in the winter, at least the city was lit up from lampposts and streetlights, and I could study the passing buildings and try not to think about how betrayed I felt inside.

"So, how'd practice go?" Dad said after a few minutes.

It was my greatest workout ever, I wanted to say. Sour words came out instead.

"You were there, weren't you?"

"Watch your tone, Josie."

I crossed my arms over my chest. "I need new grips." It was the only thing I could say out loud without crying.

"Grips?"

"Yeah. You know, for the uneven bars?"

Dad cleared his throat. "How much do grips cost?"

"I dunno. Forty dollars? Maybe fifty? There are different kinds." The stoplight turned red, and Dad slowly pressed the brake, bringing us to a full stop. An uncomfortable silence filled the air. "Forget it," I sighed, my voice barely above a whisper. "I'll see if Lucy has old ones I can use."

The light turned green, and we started driving again. "What's the latest with finding Hamlet a home?" Dad asked me lightly, changing the subject.

Like I wanted to talk about Hamlet right now, especially with him. I tucked my chin into my scarf. "No news." My words garbled from behind the soft fabric.

"I'm firm on our deal, Josie."

"Yeah, Dad. New Year's Day. I *know*."

He gave me another hard look. "I'm not sure I like your attitude tonight."

I knew I should stop snapping at him, especially since I wanted to convince him that we should keep Hamlet as a pet, but I couldn't help it tonight. All I could think about was that moment I looked up into the bleachers, hoping he saw me land my back tuck for the very first time without a spotter at my side, and saw that he wasn't even paying attention to my routine.

It's like that one little moment was poisoning everything good that had happened today, and I couldn't forgive Dad for it. I'd have given anything to turn back time, just to look up at the bleachers and see Dad's big smile and a thumbs-up.

"Did Mom tell you that Ms. Coburn is coming over for dinner on Sunday?"

"Yep, Dad. Mom told me."

Ms. Coburn was Dad's boss, and Mom had been prepping us on the Big Boss Dinner all week. *Use your manners*, Mom had instructed us. *Sarah and Ellen, no fighting. Amelia, no feeding Sugar scraps under the table, and Josie, whatever you do, make sure Hamlet is secured in her Cave!*

Later that night, after I showered and did my homework, I made a bottle of milk for Hamlet, let the piglet out of her Cave, and snuck her into the girls' bedroom. Amelia was already out cold in the bottom bunk, Ellen was downstairs reading a library book in the living room, and Sarah sat at the corner desk with headphones in her ears and a small desk lamp above her textbook, so it wasn't like anybody noticed.

I lifted Hamlet onto the ladder steps as far as I could, and it seemed as if her legs knew just what to do next. With only my hands gently supporting her, she pressed her hooves onto the rungs and climbed onto the top bunk. I quickly followed with her bottle of milk in hand, and snuggled up next to her with the covers lifted to our chins.

As I fed Hamlet her milk and felt the gentle thump of her heartbeat against my skin, the heaviness I felt inside began to lift. The piglet oinked softly into my ear as she nestled against my chest, like she was telling me everything was going to be okay, even though it didn't feel like it. I petted her head, and she slowly closed her eyes, drifting off to sleep.

I rested my head on top of hers and stared out the window, where the streetlights twinkled in the darkness, and snow began to fall lightly from the sky. The first snow of the year always feels magical, like there's this electricity buzzing through the air and anything can happen. But not this time, not this snow.

I shifted my gaze to the closed bedroom door, where faint horizontal pencil marks had been carved across the paint with various dates and names, marking each of our heights as we grew. I stared at the little dash mark next to my name and the last time I was measured, on my eleventh birthday. A sour tang filled my mouth as I imagined turning twelve and Mom's cheerful voice announcing, *"Let's get your birthday measurement!"* and Tom teasing, *"She's too tall for the door now, Ma!"*

I couldn't fight the tears any longer. I curled closer to Hamlet and she rubbed her snout against my neck, softly oinking, and I cried until my pillow was soaked from my quiet sobbing and my exhausted body sunk into the sheets.

Chapter 7

TREE DAY TRADITIONS

The next day I came home to a house smelling of cinnamon and baked apples. I dropped my backpack and
gymnastics bag on the floor and checked on Hamlet
quickly before walking to the kitchen, where Mom
stirred a wooden spoon over the stovetop. She didn't
even notice me walk in.

Invisible Josie. Typical.

"Um, *hi*," I said, pressing my palms on the countertop and boosting myself up.

"Oh! Josie! Sorry, I was just thinking about something. How's it going?"

"Fine. I'm glad it's Friday."

I hadn't told Mom about what happened the other

day with Dad, but I knew she sensed tension between us because she'd been hovering at bedtime the last few days.

You sure you're okay, Josie? she asked the first night.

Anything you want to talk about, Josie? was the second night.

Last night, she actually climbed up the bunk bed ladder—which she never does anymore—and planted a big kiss on my forehead. "Are you worried about Hamlet, JoJo?" she asked quietly.

I just nodded, because I *was* worried about Hamlet, but I was worried about lots of other things, too. "She's a nice little pig," Mom said, smiling. "Remember how Lou's mom said it was good for Hamlet to hang out with other animals?" I nodded again. She leaned forward onto my down comforter, lowering her voice. "Well, don't tell your father, but I've been letting Hamlet loose in the house sometimes before my afternoon shift at the Community Center."

"*Really?*" I grinned.

"Really. She follows me all around the house, right at my heels like a puppy."

"Yeah." I hadn't been able to stop smiling. "She gets attached to people like that."

"She does seem to have a good heart." Mom had planted another big kiss on my forehead and said, "Night night, sweetie. Tomorrow's a big day."

But come to think of it, I hadn't asked *why*, I was so consumed with imagining Hamlet exploring the house while I was sitting in Language Arts class.

But now that I was home from school the next day, I was curious. Big Day?

"What're you doing?" I leaned toward the open pot, sniffing. "Ohhhhhh, it's apple cider! Can I have some?"

Mom frowned. "You know I don't like you girls sitting on the counters."

"But there's no place to sit in here," I protested, waving my arms around our tiny kitchen. We didn't have bar stools, like at Lucy's place. Mom reached for a ladle, scooped steaming cider and mulled spices out of the pot, and poured it into a thermos. She spun the top on nice and tight and handed it to me. The warmth of the thermos felt good against the cracked blisters on my palms.

"How was gymnastics practice?"

I unscrewed the top of the thermos and gently blew cool air into it. "Pretty good."

"You thanked Lucy's mom for the ride . . . ?"

"Yes, Mom. It was no big deal." Lucy's family gave me rides all the time, so it really wasn't. Besides, we had worked hard on vault today, so we had lots to talk about after our workout.

"I CAN'T FIND IT!" yelled a voice from upstairs.

Mom turned toward the stairwell and yelled back, "KEEP LOOKING!" Then she glanced my way before sprinkling some nutmeg powder over the pot. "Your hair looks cute."

"Thanks. The Level Seven girls taught us how to do fishtail braids." I twisted the top back on the thermos and pressed my lips against it, tentatively taking a sip from the hole at the top. The sweet, warm tang of apples and cinnamon burst across my tongue. I started to pull an arm out of my coat, but Mom stopped me.

"Keep your coat on," she said with a knowing smile.

"Why—what's going on?" I looked at her suspiciously. Tom's football game was tomorrow, so it couldn't be that. A series of loud oinks reached my ears, and I felt my face twist in horror. "No, Mom, not Hamlet—"

"No, honey. Not Hamlet, don't worry. Although she's been making quite the racket, so I think she needs a walk." Mom turned off the stove and poured the rest of the cider into her own large travel mug. "It's Tree Day!"

I felt my face light up. Tree Day wasn't a national holiday or anything, but it was one in the Shilling household. It's the day we cut down a Christmas tree from a nearby farm and decorate it in our living room.

I jumped off the counter. "Yay! Where is everybody?"

"Dad and the older girls went to shovel the van out. It's parked a few blocks over, so we have about ten minutes. One of Amelia's mittens has gone missing again. Have you seen it?"

"The purple striped ones? Those are *mine.*" I threw my hands in the air. "Ugh! She's *always* taking my stuff without permission and then losing something. If Millie just learned to *put things back where they belong.* . . ." I exhaled, releasing my frustration with my breath, the way Coach had been teaching us. It was Tree Day, one of the best days of the year! I couldn't be annoyed with my little sister today. "Fine. She can borrow my mittens. My hands are plenty warm now." I held up my hot thermos. "I'll go take Hamlet out now." I emphasized the words, so Mom would see how responsible I was being.

"Great, thank you, Josie." Mom walked toward the stairway, calling over her shoulder, "FIVE-MINUTE WARNING! Millie, grab Josie the old red mittens!" Mom moved to her purse resting on the hall table and pulled out her white wool hat. "Take Sugar with you, okay, Josie?"

Hamlet wiggled as soon as she saw me round the corner. The lower half of her body was tucked beneath the unfolded Sports section of *City Centennial*, so she looked like a rustling newspaper. She oinked happily, and I reached down while she jumped up on her hind legs. "Hi, Hammie. I'm happy to see you, too. Ah ah ah! No jumping." I shifted the baby gate to the side. She nestled her warm body against my legs, snout lifted eagerly toward my thermos.

"No way, Hamlet!" I yanked my arm away, out of her reach. She pushed her way against me again, snorting, jumping on my legs. She was not only hungry, she had energy to burn off! "Careful, Hammie!" I said. "It's *hot* cider. Now let's get your leash. . . ."

Even though we live in a bustling city, the beginning of winter can bring a quietness with it, which makes the world seem like it's on pause. By this time of year, the trees are barren of their leaves, and the plants seem to fall asleep.

A thin blanket of fresh snow coated our patio set. The black of Amelia's bike tires now looked white, and I was careful to watch my step for the garden hose, which I couldn't see on the ground anymore, but I knew it was around here somewhere. Sugar padded around the yard off leash, her snout pressed down, as if she was suddenly interested in what might be hiding beneath the layer of snow.

I followed Hamlet and Sugar, just listening to the soft crunch of my boots on the frozen dead grass and pretended I was walking on the balance beam, heels angled in and toes pointed out.

Step, step, step—Ta-da!

I raised my right arm high above my head. I had just two weeks until our team gymnastics meet. *Practice your posture every single day*, Coach had told us. *Shoulders back. Chin lifted. Visualize your routines!*

Hamlet tugged me toward a tree stump, and I watched as she rooted her snout into a pile of snow. I felt a shiver trickle down my spine, and I knew it wasn't from the cold wind.

I only had a few weeks to convince my parents we should keep Hamlet, too.

I couldn't fail in either mission. But I needed more time.

As we walked along the fence we shared with Mrs. Taglioni, I gripped Hamlet's leash more tightly in my hands. Hamlet was growing so quickly, and every day her tugging felt stronger than the day before.

I hadn't seen Mrs. Taglioni since that day I told her we were pet sitting a puppy. That probably made her happy. I scowled, looking over at where her townhouse came into view. The gutters were scraped clean of leaves, and the house siding had a bright blue paint, which wasn't peeling off or anything. Mrs. Taglioni was probably inside now, hanging out with her cat and sugar gliders and polishing thumbprints off her spectacles.

Whatever. That was just fine with me. I was glad I hadn't bumped into her, either.

I spun a half-turn and raised my left arm to the sky. My muscles felt sore from yesterday's conditioning— push-ups and pull-ups—but it felt good to be gaining strength.

Back inside, Amelia pulled knee-high socks over her jeans.

"That looks ridiculous," I told my little sister.

"What? They're waterproof!"

Sometimes it takes us Shillings a whole ten minutes to get out the door. But today I didn't sulk on the couch. Instead, I tucked Hamlet back into her Cave and secured the baby gate in front of it, and then waited patiently on the front stoop until Dad honked the horn from the van out front. We were off!

The tree farm was a twenty-minute drive outside the city. It smelled fresh like pine needles and as earthy as garden soil, and it felt about fifty degrees colder than in our backyard. My boots sunk into deep snow out here, too.

I took another sip of my still-warm cider as we wandered through the trees. Almost immediately, Sarah and Ellen decided on different trees. They rarely agreed on anything these days.

"But Dad, this is a *Douglas fir*," Ellen said, as if it was the most obvious thing in the world. "Its needles won't drop as fast. Who wants to sweep up needles every day? Good luck with a blue spruce. And it's not even fragrant, Sarah. Isn't that the whole point of *live* Christmas trees? We might as well buy an artificial tree if we get that thing." Ellen made a face at Sarah, who was examining the branches of a nearby tree.

"Whatever, Dragon Face," Sarah said, scowling back.

"Why don't you go hang out with Trisha with that

attitude?" Ellen countered. "And besides, you'd like the dragon book if you *gave it a chance*."

"Sarah! Don't call your sister names," scolded Mom. "And Ellen, this is Tree Day. Of course we want Sarah here with us."

"And we're not buying an artificial tree," added Dad, scratching his chin. "So let's see. Douglas fir, or blue spruce?"

Dad moved to circle the Douglas fir, bumping right into me. "Oh! Sorry, Josie. Didn't see you there."

"Typical," I muttered, crossing my arms in front of my chest. It was a miracle they remembered to invite me to Tree Day.

"Both are lovely trees," chimed in Mom. "It's a tough decision. . . ."

Amelia leaned forward to give the spruce needles a good whiff, but ended up getting too close and pricking her nose on a branch. "Ow!" she cried. "The needles aren't soft either. I like Ellen's tree better."

"I rest my case," Ellen said. Sarah sighed, let go of the tree branch, and wrapped her arms around her waist in defeat.

Dad watched my older sisters closely. "Be kind to your sister, Ellen."

"We bought a Douglas fir last year, too, Dad, remember?" Ellen said. "It's not only tradition, it makes more sense."

"Let's vote!" said Amelia.

Sarah rolled her eyes. "Tom's not here so we can't vote. No fair."

I threw my hands up in the air. "Doesn't anyone care what *I* think?"

Ellen gave Sarah's tree a once-over again. "That one's too tall for the living room, anyway. It'll scrape paint off the ceiling."

Maybe Ellen was right about the trees, and maybe Sarah had a permanent attitude problem, but still. My heart ached a little as I watched Sarah weave through the rows of tree varieties, disappearing from view.

"Stay close, Sarah!" called Mom. "It's dark out!"

Dad waved down one of the workers to help him chop down the Douglas fir. Ellen untwisted the price tag off one of its branches while she told Amelia other facts about the tree, like how old she thought it might be and how it reminded her of this magical evergreen forest that housed elves in a book she read once.

"I'm going to walk around," I said, and before Mom

could remind me, I added, "I know, *I know*, I won't go far!"

I broke into a run without knowing exactly where I was going—only who I wanted to find. I finally spotted Sarah's ponytail swishing a few yards ahead. My sister didn't stop walking, but she kicked snow high up in the air with every step, so it only took me a minute to catch up with her.

"Hey! The spruce was pretty," I offered. Sarah didn't look at me. *Stomp, stomp.* I tried again. "Did you try Mom's cider yet?"

Sarah sighed and reached for my thermos. She took a sip and then licked her lips. "Tastes more like watered-down cookies, shortcake."

"There're cinnamon sticks on the bottom, okay? Sheesh!" I grabbed for it back, but Sarah broke into a grin. "And stop calling me 'shortcake.' Maybe we don't like your mean nicknames, okay?"

"Can't you take a joke?"

Sarah didn't understand that sometimes her sarcasm was *exhausting*. I looked toward the angled glass roof-top of a nearby greenhouse. It practically glowed in the darkness. "You can't blame Ellen for the tree thing, you know," I said. "It's not like you're the easiest person to get along with. Sometimes it's hard to know how to talk to you."

Sarah glared at me. "I didn't ask your opinion."

I waved my arms around me. "You have such an attitude problem! You're ruining Tree Day!"

"I'M NOT TRYING TO RUIN ANYTHING!"

Her anger caught us both off guard. I took a step backward, and Sarah's eyes met mine. Hers had turned almost glossy, like cat eyes. She was about to cry, I suddenly realized.

Sarah.

My older sister, who never cried about anything.

I drew in the crisp, fresh air and exhaled slowly. "You don't need to be mad all the time," I whispered.

"Ha. Easy for you to say." The words choked up in her throat. "You're not the invisible one in the family."

I couldn't help it, but I busted out laughing, even though Sarah was barely holding it together, and she never opened up to me, ever, ever, ever.

"I feel like I am!" I told her. "Trust me. *All the time.*"

She clutched the thermos in her hands. "You do?"

"Totally. Mom forgot I was in the room like twice today."

Sarah cracked a smile, but something caught her eye and it quickly faded from her face. "Josie," my sister gasped. "Your *hands*. What happened to your skin? They're all raw and busted up."

"Oh. That." I slipped my cold hands into my coat pockets and shrugged off her comment, pretending that my palms hadn't been burning fire for two days and I hadn't been applying wound-healing cream on them every night before bed. "My grips wore out so I started wearing Lucy's old ones. They're just a little small, that's all. Now come on, Douglas fir or not, it's *our* tree and it'll be great no matter what. Let's go!"

Sarah stood for a second in silence, just staring at me. Finally, she reached down to the ground and scooped up a handful of powder snow. She chucked the snowball at me, hitting me square in the chest. "Bet ya can't hit me back!" she cried gleefully, breaking into a sprint in the other direction.

Usually I'd be really careful about running through the darkness and throwing snowballs. I mean, what if I sprained an ankle, or broke a finger? I'd be doomed. And I wasn't even wearing gloves!

But it was Tree Day, and Sarah was actually talking to me like a real person and not just an annoying little sister, and snow began to fall from the night sky, and that made everything just a teeny bit different.

So I bolted after her through the trees.

It was the only time I'd ever had a snowball fight in the middle of a tree farm, and with Sarah of all people. When the powdery snowballs burst against the branches above us, it was like watching a cascade of shooting stars.

Chapter 8

IT'S BEGINNING TO LOOK A LOT LIKE CHRISTMAS

Someone thrust the front door wide open just as we were carefully unwrapping all the Christmas decoration boxes.

"Tom!" Mom cried, waving a popcorn garland. The family cheered. "I didn't think you could make it this weekend!"

"Got a ride after class with an old high school friend," Tom said with a grin. "They'll take me back in the morning for the home game. I got your message on the answering machine. You didn't think I'd miss Tree Day, did you?"

"Of course not." Mom gave him a big hug. "And look at our beautiful tree! It's a Douglas fir."

Tom nodded in approval. "Yeah, a nice big fluffy one. Last year's was like crunched on one side, remember? It had sad branches."

"Here—we're just getting started." Dad offered Tom an unopened cardboard box. My brother took a seat next to me on the couch and peeled back the aged masking tape.

"Nutcracker dudes! Love these guys." Tom ripped off the bubble wrap, handing it over to Amelia, who we all knew would never pass up the chance to pop bubble wrap. *Snap! Snap!*

"The Little Drummer Boy" blared through the radio speakers. Dad untangled a box of string lights while Tom caught us up on the latest college and football news. Ellen updated everyone on her Georgetown University application and how she met the criteria for three scholarships, and Sarah shared that she couldn't wait for the PSAT to be over. Amelia told us about how yesterday she and Lou were throwing tennis balls out back, and they got Hamlet to catch one with her mouth, just like Sugar could, and I asked her three times if she'd put Hamlet on a leash, like she knows she's supposed to. She even promised that she'd park her bike by the gate after the snow melted.

"So, JoJo. How's gymnastics going?" Tom asked, turning to me. I unwrapped a sparkly mermaid ornament from a ball of newspaper while "Silent Night" played in the background.

"Okay, I guess."

"Really?" Tom's voice rose in pitch. "I hope you thought long and hard about what we talked about—"

"*Shhhhh!*"

I shot my brother a scolding look. That conversation was just between us. I wasn't ready to broadcast all my gymnastics problems to the whole family. Not yet, at least.

Dad's cell phone rang from the side table, but he didn't reach for it. Instead, he kept a firm grip on the tree trunk as he tightened it into the tree stand. "Sarah, can you grab a cup of water to feed the tree?"

Mom and Sarah helped pour a jug of water into the tree stand and tightened up the screws around the trunk until the tree was straight and secure. Ellen handed Dad the lights, helping him thread the wire around the tree branches.

"Josie nailed a back tuck a few days ago," Amelia piped up, hanging a pinecone ornament on a tree branch.

I felt my cheeks burn with heat. "Who told you that?"

"Lucy." Amelia glanced my way. I must've been scowling because she said, *"What?"*

Dad peeked through the pine needle branches. "You can do a back tuck, Josie?"

You would've known if you watched my practice, I wanted to say.

"Yeah," I said instead.

"Wow, Josie. That's really impressive!" Dad grinned. "I'm so proud of you."

"Will we get to see you do it at your gymnastics meet in two weeks?" asked Mom.

I shrugged, like it was no big deal. "Yeah."

"Can't wait." Dad's voice was muffled from behind the tree. "It's been on my calendar for months."

I didn't realize he even knew about my gymnastics meet, or that he'd written anything about me on his calendar *ever.*

Dad twisted the lights around another branch and belted into song, *"In the meadow you can build a snowman . . ."* I felt a slow smile creep over my face. Sarah stared at me like she wanted to say something but was holding back. I didn't press her on it, either. Because for the first time in a long time, us Shillings were actually *talking* to each other. And not just talking—*listening*.

Dad's cell phone rang again. "Don't you need to get that, Stephen?" Mom's eyebrows pinched together. "It could be—"

"No work on holidays, remember?" Dad broke in with a smile, popping his head out from behind the tree again. "Hey, who wants eggnog?"

"I do!" Ellen and I said in unison.

"*Ohhhh*, the Popsicle ornament!" Amelia cried out in surprise. "I want to hang this one in front."

Mom hummed along to "Rocking Around the Christmas Tree," and my brother said, "Tree dude needs a name, guys." Tom leaned back on the couch as if he was exhausted after just opening a few ornaments. I caught the sparkle of his stud earring in the light. "I can't call him Tree anymore. It just doesn't feel right. He's one of us now."

"What about Doug?" Sarah suggested. "Or Fur?"

Tom pinched his eyebrows together in thought. "He does look like a Doug." Sarah laughed, and even Ellen cracked a grin.

"Awww, look at Hamlet and Sugar!" Amelia cooed, pointing.

We all turned to see the two animals snuggled up in front of the crackling fire. I hadn't realized that Hamlet wasn't in her Cave. Someone must've let her out, because she'd never gotten out on her own before. But there she was, snoring quietly next to Sugar.

They were lying side by side on the living room rug, and Hamlet rested her pink snout on top of Sugar's reddish-brown back. Light from the fireplace cast shadows across the pig's and dog's bodies. Their eyes were closed. Hamlet's chest swelled with a big breath and slowly deflated as she exhaled a relaxed sigh. Seeing her little hoof next to Sugar's furry paw brought a smile to my face.

Sticking out from under Hamlet's body was something blue. My pulse skyrocketed. *Dad's blue slippers!* Oh no! Not today, on Tree Day, of all days! I bolted upright from my seated position by the tree and started toward the fireplace.

"Let her be, Josie," Dad said gently, stopping me in my tracks.

"But—um—Dad—"

He reassured me with a smile. "It's Tree Day, honey. I'll cut Hamlet some slack. We'll wash them tomorrow."

I nodded, feeling a warmth radiate in my chest. "Sure, Dad." My brother flashed me a lazy grin, and I knew he was thinking the same thing as me.

Anything can happen on Tree Day.

We decorated our little city townhouse until twinkly garlands stretched across the drapes, the fleece Santa blanket was splayed across the back of the couch, praying ceramic angels lined our living room windowsill, each stocking hung from the fireplace, a star rested on top of the tree, and the very last ornament, a shiny green glass pickle, waited on the coffee table. I picked it up delicately and handed it to Sarah.

"Pickle always goes last," I said. "It's tradition."

"You can do it," Sarah said, but I could tell in her eyes that a piece of her wanted to receive the greatest honor of Tree Day.

I looked around at my family, and they all watched me with eager eyes. I shook my head. "You should do it," I said.

Sarah grinned and took the pickle from me. As she moved toward a branch on the tree, Tom waved his arms in protest.

"Wait! Wait!" Tom said. "This is my favorite

Christmas jam! Turn it up. We need an appropriate soundtrack for this."

Ellen spun the volume dial on the radio until "Dominick the Donkey" blasted through the speakers so loudly that Mrs. Taglioni was probably grumbling into her hot tea next door.

"Jiggety jig, it's *Dominick . . . the . . . Donkey!*" Tom sang at the top of his lungs.

"*This* is your favorite holiday song?" Mom laughed.

"Figures," said Sarah with a laugh.

Amelia joined in singing, pretending her clenched fist was a microphone. Sugar barked, and Hamlet sprung to her hooves, wriggling her way next to me to lick my arm. Mom jingled her house keys like sleigh bells, Dad and Ellen clapped their hands, and I laughed until my belly ached. Sarah studied the tree and finally grabbed a branch, sliding the wire loop of the pickle ornament onto the Douglas fir, all while my brother chanted "Hee haw! HEE HAW!" until he was red in the face.

It was only when Dad turned off the lights and we stood there in the darkness of the living room, staring at our Christmas tree lit up in red, blue, green, and white lights, that someone turned off the music. My brother unwrapped a candy cane and sighed happily, "Doug looks good, guys."

Snow danced outside the window, but it felt like that winter calm had come inside the house, too, even if just for one night.

Chapter 9

THE THREE-WEEK RULE

The letter burned a hole in my pocket.

Okay. It didn't *really* burn a hole, but the knowledge that it was there, just waiting to be handed over to my parents, ignited something like a fire inside of me.

I'd opened and read it, of course. My name was on the envelope so it wasn't like I was doing anything wrong. The letter was from the gymnastics center, reminding my parents that my team registration fee was due by January 1st. *Two hundred whole dollars.*

I walked home from the library, slowly inhaling and exhaling, like I do at practice when trying to visualize a goal. The fee was a lot of money, but I had saved $76.02 in allowance just for this moment. Plus, I was *this* close to winning the vegetarian bet with Lucy, which would be another forty dollars if I pulled through. Grandma usually gave me some money for the holidays, so hopefully I'd only have to ask my parents for fifty dollars or so. Still a lot of money, but not so bad. If I could show my parents that I made sacrifices on my end, too, that I was saving instead of buying things my friends were buying like apps, leggings, and books, then they'd see how important the team was to me.

With each step I walked, it felt as if the letter seared into my jeans, reminding me of what would happen if I couldn't pay up by New Year's Day.

I had twenty-eight days left to figure it out.

I kicked my boots through a slushy puddle as I worked through my thoughts. Yesterday had been so busy with Tom's football game, playing with Hamlet, and gymnastics practice, I was lucky that no one else got the mail first after it was dropped through the mail slot in our front door.

I'd tell Mom about the letter after the holidays, when things calmed down—*definitely* not today: Dad's boss was coming over for dinner.

"Hey, Josie," said a voice. I stopped in my tracks. Sully was waiting on our stoop, his investigator notebook open.

"Oh, hey!" I said in surprise. We usually met on his front stoop, not mine, and I wasn't aware of a stoops meeting. "Are you looking for Trisha?" I asked. His older sister had been hanging out with Sarah lately.

Sully shook his head. "I've been thinking about your pig problem. . . ."

It felt like my stomach did a somersault. I didn't like thinking of Hamlet as a problem—but I guess she was. "Yeah?"

"And something came to me. . . ." He tapped the eraser to his chin. "Hamlet's been with you, what, two weeks now, right?"

I nodded. "One and a half."

"So I have this theory—I call it the Three-Week Rule. I think that it takes people three weeks to get used to things. Sometimes they even change their minds about stuff, too. Last month the twins' mom went on this sugar-free diet kick. . . . It was called Paleo Something. Did they tell you about it?"

"I have no idea what you're talking about." I crossed my arms in front of my chest. "What does this have to do with Hamlet, anyway?"

"I'm getting there! So, Carlos used to complain about it *all the time* in History class that the only sugar they were allowed from now on was fruit. And since school doesn't serve cookies or anything at lunchtime, it was like Carlos just *couldn't* get his hands on sugar no matter how badly he wanted it. . . . But then last week something weird happened. After gym class, Denny was passing around lollipops, and when he offered one to Carlos, he didn't want it."

"Maybe Carlos doesn't like lollipops?" I said, but as soon as the words left my mouth, I knew that wasn't true. I'd definitely seen Carlos have a lollipop before.

"Na-ah . . . I asked him. He said he didn't want sugar anymore, that he'd just gotten used to not having it. Like it wasn't a big deal."

"Carlos not eating sugar and keeping a pig in the city are very different things," I told Sully. "Besides. What about Fernanda?"

"What about her?"

"Wasn't she off sugar, too? Did Fernanda eat a lollipop?"

"She's not in my gym class, so I don't know. But *now* you're thinking like an investigator." Sully spun a few pages back in his Case File notebook. He tapped his pencil on a scribbled list, which from my angle looked like a calendar. "According to my notes, I haven't witnessed the twins eat sugar for three weeks."

I sat down on the stoop next to Sully. "I still don't know what this has to do with Hamlet."

"Okay." He tipped back the brim of his ball cap. "Another example. Your brother came home with a pierced ear on Thanksgiving, right?"

"Yeah?"

"Well. Did your parents ever make him take it out?"

I pinched my lips together, remembering seeing his earring at Tree Day. "Um . . . no. My parents stopped being mad, and I guess we all just sorta forgot about it."

Sully grinned. "This is the turning point in the Case for Keeping Hamlet. Your folks are getting more attached to Hamlet every day. They're not going to want to give her up! Trust me on this. The Three-Week Rule."

I stared at Sully's case notebook, thinking. "Well, Dad *did* let Hamlet sleep on his slippers the other day . . . and Mom told me that she's been letting Hamlet out of her Cave sometimes when we're at school, before her shift at the Community Center. . . ."

"Aha!" Sully did a fist pump in the air. "See, I'm right!"

Snow began to fall, lightly at first, and then much

harder, like someone was sweeping it off the rooftops. "I gotta go inside," I told him. "We have this dinner thing, and I promised that I'd clean Hamlet's Cave and do my homework first."

I didn't tell Sully that caring for Hamlet took a lot more time than I had originally anticipated. Every time I cleaned her Cave, I had to remove the old newspapers, scrub the floor tiles with cleaner, lay down new papers and cedar chips, and then change her litter box. It felt like I was constantly refilling her water and pouring in another scoop of dry pellet feed into her food bowl. And now that Hamlet was getting older and bigger, she seemed to have more energy, too. I had to walk her outside three or four times a day so she could get her wiggles out!

I got to my feet and hopped up the stoop steps. Even on this side of the door, I could hear the house phone ringing. I started to spin the doorknob, but Sully called out, "Josie, wait!"

I spun around. Sully stood just a few feet away from me, and I realized that he was actually a lot taller then I remembered. Maybe he was having a growth spurt, too.

"Heard you got a back tuck," he said.

I couldn't stop grinning, because the truth was, I *did*

get my back tuck. I'd done it perfectly every workout since that first time. A few days ago I would've asked Sully who blabbed the news to him: was it Lucy, or Amelia? But maybe it was the magic of Tree Day still lingering in my heart, or maybe it was that I was feeling more confident in my skills, because I didn't blush or hunch over or look away, like I might've done a week ago. Instead, I lifted my chin and kept on grinning.

"Sure did," I said. *Ring ring! Ring ring!* echoed in the distance, but I barely heard it.

Sully shook the snow off his hat. "That's really awesome."

"Thanks."

He flopped his hat back on his head and grinned again. "Three-Week Rule!"

I watched as Sully turned down the street, past the twins' place, and up the steps of his townhouse, where a large menorah sat on the windowsill, glowing with six blue lights.

"You won't forget?" he called out.

I suddenly felt lightheaded, but I wasn't sure why. "Nope!" I yelled back, waving. "See ya, Sully! And Happy Hanukkah!"

He grinned. My face flushed pink, and I zoomed

inside the house, slamming the door closed, and pressed the back of my head against the frame.

Ring ring!

Ring ring!

I snapped back to reality. Hadn't the phone been ringing for a while already? Where *was* everybody? Dad's boss would be here soon.

I rushed to the phone hanging on the kitchen wall. "Hello?" I said breathlessly, dropping the mail on the countertop and double-checking that my registration letter was safely tucked away in my pocket.

"Josie? Sarah?"

It took me a second to recognize the voice on the other end of the line. "Oh! Dr. Stern? It's Josie."

"Yes, hi there, Josie. How are you?"

"Great! Are you looking for Lou? I don't think he's here."

"Oh, no, thank you. Lou's upstairs in his room now. I'm actually calling about Hamlet. I'm glad I reached you."

I spun around, trying to get a better look into Hamlet's Cave. I could barely see her from this angle. Maybe she had burrowed under the newspapers. "Is everything okay?"

"Yes, everything's okay! I just wanted to let you know that Hamlet's blood tests came back negative and assure you she seems perfectly healthy."

I tried to stretch the phone cord as far as I could to get a better look at Hamlet. It looked like her head was bobbing up and down, the way it does when she's flipping an ear of corn around to eat all the good parts.

"Okay, well, that's good!" I said, breathing a sigh of relief.

Reason #7 for the Case for Keeping Hamlet: She's a Very Healthy Pig.

"Now," she continued, "I want to speak with your parents about this, too, but I have a friend out in Zanesville who may be interested in taking Hamlet off your hands. . . ."

I felt my heart skip a beat. Hamlet had barely just gotten here—I wasn't ready to give her up! Plus, I was still working on my parents. What if Sully's Three-Week Rule was right and I just needed another week or so for them to become attached to her?

I needed to stall Dr. Stern!

"Um." I twisted the phone cord around my finger. "They want her as a pet pig, right?"

"For the time being."

My breath caught. "So only in the beginning? And then what?"

"It'd be more of a trial basis, Josie," she said.

"Um. I'm not sure." This was happening too fast. My hands began to shake just imagining someone coming to our house to take her. No! "I'll think about it, okay? Thanks so much for calling—"

"Josie, I know how attached you are to Hamlet," she broke in. "But trust me, they're a very nice family and Hamlet would be lucky to live on their farm. As long as the pig doesn't show any aggression toward humans, they will keep her as a companion for their other barn animals. They're willing to come by in the next week or two and pick her up. They don't live in one of those farms outside the city—they're a bit further out. Your father didn't answer his cell, and I was hoping to speak with your parents about this tonight. Are they around?"

My heart began to race. *This week or next?* No way. I needed to focus on my routines—I couldn't worry about this right now!

Right then I spotted a note taped to the door of the fridge: *Josie, I went on a quick grocery store run with Amelia.*

Ellen and Sarah will be home soon from the library. Dad's on his way . . . Please finish your chores & see you in a bit! Love, Mom.

"We're having company tonight for dinner, so they'll be back soon," I told Dr. Stern. "I'll let them know you called." Right then I overheard Lou yelling in the background, something about being a ninja. Hi-*YAH!*

"Okay, thank you—*Lou, wait one moment, I'm on the phone!*—Good-bye, Josie. Please don't forget."

"I won't."

We hung up the phone and I wandered over to Hamlet's Cave. Math homework could wait. Right now I had a million things to think about. I climbed over the baby gate, where Hamlet's face was pressed to the ground. She spun around to greet me, oinking loudly and licking my legs.

Her snout was soaked!

"Hamlet!" I scolded her. She had flipped over her water bowl, and the layers of newspapers on the floor were drenched. "Scooch over," I said, and she lowered her head, the way Sugar does when we catch her napping on the couch and she feels guilty.

I pulled up all the wet newspapers and tossed them, retrieved a roll of paper towels from the kitchen and soaked up the excess water on the floor. After I dried off Hamlet's hooves and snout, I laid down a fresh layer of newspapers and curled up next to the pig on the floor.

"Oh, Hammie," I said, scratching behind her ears. "I'm going to have to wait to give you more water until dinnertime. I can't risk you flipping your bowl again when Ms. Coburn is here!"

Hamlet oinked and wiggled up next to my chest, where she likes to hear my heartbeat. We lay there for a minute, just listening to each other, while I worked through the worries on my heart. I knew I should finish up my homework and get ready for our dinner guest, but I felt so drained of energy.

Will my parents pay the gymnastics registration fee?

Is there a chance Hamlet will be taken away from us?

I should be focusing on my gymnastics meet, but now I had *two* big things to tell my parents. And I didn't want to talk to them about either one.

Chapter 10

BIG BOSS DINNER

I tried my best to be pleasant, but Dad's boss—Angela Coburn—had an opinion about *everything*. Our Christmas tree was too colorful and gave her a headache (we turned off Doug's lights). The crab cakes were too hot (Dad brought them back into the kitchen to cool). The house was too cold (Ellen cranked up the heat).

I promised Mom that I'd keep Hamlet in her Cave, but then Amelia blabbed the news to Ms. Coburn—*of course*—so when she asked to see the pig, even Dad couldn't say no.

Hamlet was much heavier now and harder to control in my arms, but she didn't start kicking me with her hooves until Ms. Coburn leaned closer to her, examining the pig like she was a cell under a microscope in Science class.

"Hmmm." Ms. Coburn frowned, deepening the wrinkles around her mouth.

I wasn't quite sure what *hmmm* meant, but I could tell from the way Dad coughed into his closed fist that it wasn't a good thing.

"The crab cakes should be cool by now," Dad said. "Why don't we go take a seat in the living room?"

"Yay!" cheered my little sister. She turned to Ms. Coburn. "We never get to eat crab cakes. Only on special occasions."

"Yeah, my dad's crab cakes are the best!" I added, hoping the conversation didn't steer toward Hamlet. As they moved down the hall, I carefully set the pig back down in her Cave. I understood how it felt to have people snickering about me, too, and I wanted her to know that she was a good pig. It wasn't her fault that some humans just aren't animal people.

"Guess boss lady isn't really into pigs," I whispered to her, giving her a pat on the head. She lifted my hand with her snout, making me laugh.

Looking down at Hamlet now, I was amazed by how

big she looked. In pig years, she could've been a teenager! Her Cave used to be the perfect size, but now it was getting harder for her to turn her body around and comfortably lie down.

I gave her another pat. "I'll come back and check on you later."

I washed up and returned to the living room, listening to Ms. Coburn drone on and on about her son who had recently moved to Chicago and gotten an important job at a law firm.

"Oh, you must be so proud," Mom said. "Shrimp cocktail?"

I looked at the bored expressions on my sisters' faces and considered retreating back to Hamlet's Cave, but Mom called us to the table. The sweet aroma of onion soup, baked bread, and meatloaf caught my nose. My stomach growled. I'd been so busy this afternoon I'd barely eaten anything! I couldn't touch the meatloaf, but at least the soup and bread were fine. I'd sneak some cheese out of the fridge later if I was still hungry.

Mom had secretly assigned our seats before Ms. Coburn arrived so that she would feel "more comfortable." Us girls were supposed to sit on one end of the table and the adults on the other. But somehow we got all switched around, and Ms. Coburn took the seat next to me. A little groan escaped my mouth, and Mom must've overheard it because she narrowed her eyes at me. *Whoops.*

Out of all the kids, Ellen handled our guest the best. When Ms. Coburn talked about quality control issues surrounding a recent toothpaste reformulation, Ellen seemed to understand some of the unusual terms that sounded like a different language to me, words like *sourcing* and *recall.*

"It's good to see your daughter has a strong, curious mind," said Ms. Coburn, nodding toward Ellen in approval, as if Sarah, Amelia, and I weren't even in the room. "Reminds me of myself when I was young. What are your plans after graduation?"

Ellen sat up straight. Talking about life after high school was one of her favorite subjects. "I just sent off my college applications."

Ms. Coburn tugged at the sleeves of her sweater, right along her wrists. "Hope we can count on you to be a Buckeye," she said to my sister.

It wasn't a question. Ellen's face turned a slight shade of pink, but instead of explaining why, Sarah chimed in. "Yeah, right! Ellen hates the Buckeyes."

"Hmm." Ms. Coburn's eyes narrowed, giving my sisters and me a once-over, as if we were all traitors as well.

"I don't *hate the Buckeyes*, Sarah," Ellen said through clenched teeth. Then she turned to Ms. Coburn. "I'm hoping I'll get into Columbia. Er"—she met eyes with my mom—"on scholarship. They have an excellent English program. I want to be a book editor."

"Book editor?" Ms. Coburn almost choked on a sip of wine. "Why on earth would you want to do that? We need more strong, smart women in the business world. That's where you should focus your efforts—not on literary nonsense."

"But Ellen likes dragons!" Amelia said. "And princesses, but only if they have swords, because she never wanted to watch *Sleeping Beauty* with me. But we did make my gingerbread house more of a gingerbread *castle* this year. There's even gumdrop dragons near the front door."

"Gumdrop dragons, hmm." Ms. Coburn shook her head in disapproval, and my oldest sister's face turned bright red.

"Dr. Stern is a super strong smart woman," Amelia continued. "She neuters and picks up poop and diagnoses cancer, and once she even removed a sock from an esophagus!"

Ms. Coburn coughed into her napkin. "And Dr. Stern is . . . ?"

Amelia beamed. "Our vet. She's my best friend's mom!"

"Cheese?" Dad returned from the kitchen, and Mom's tight expression softened in relief. Dad passed around the platter of baked bread, cheese, and fruit— and not just the regular orange cheese, either, that comes in the clear little plastic wrappers: these were fancy white cheeses with peppers in them, and fruits that we never ever get to eat, like pineapple and mango, and fresh-baked bread that I know my mom picked out special just for tonight.

"I'm off simple carbs," said Ms. Coburn, waving her fingers over the bread before grabbing the serving fork and spearing herself a pineapple wedge.

"Oh?" Dad said in a forced light tone.

"Can I eat my gingerbread castle now?" asked Amelia, crossing her arms over her chest.

"Growing food first, Millie, you know the rules," said Mom with a smile. Then she turned to Dad's boss.

"So, any holiday plans, Angela?"

"I always spend a few weeks at my house on Buckeye Lake," Ms. Coburn said.

"A few weeks? Really." Mom unfolded her napkin on her lap. I wondered if she was thinking what I was thinking—that it'd be super nice to go to a lake house for a few weeks. We never get to take vacations like that.

"Have you been before?" Ms. Coburn looked around the table, like we were parasites and not real people.

Mom passed around the salad bowl. "Not as a family, but Sarah, didn't you visit Buckeye Lake with one of your school friends, sweetie? Last summer, maybe?" My sister nodded, but she kept her mouth shut, which was probably for the best.

"Then you probably saw our house," said Ms. Coburn, reaching for the salad tongs. "The biggest on the lake. Made sure of it when it was built. Don't want a bunch of ruffians to take over the area." She grabbed the saltshaker and hovered it over her lettuce. *Shake, shake.*

"What's a ruffian?" asked Amelia, cocking her head sideways. Sarah kicked her foot underneath the table. "Ow! What was *that* for?"

"More bread?" Mom gave the plate a little shove across the table and Amelia snatched up an end piece, always her favorite, and that shut her right up.

An awkward silence followed. I desperately wanted Dad to fill it with reassuring words, but he didn't. He seemed just as uncomfortable as the rest of us.

When Mom placed a bowl of onion soup in front of me, I was lost in my thoughts and started slurping it up right away.

"Good soup, Mom!" said Amelia. I rolled my eyes. She wasn't even eating it, she was just swirling her spoon around, creating a big whirlpool inside the bowl. She was probably hoping Mom would break off a piece of her gingerbread castle as a reward.

"Yes, delicious!" Ms. Coburn agreed, rubbing her lips together in thought. "Is this beef broth, Emily? You must give me the recipe." She reached for the salt-shaker again. *Shake, shake.*

"Pepper?" Sarah offered, a smirk on her face.

My spoon clinked against the bowl. Tears stung my eyes. I looked at Mom, my eyes wide with concern.

"There's beef in this soup?" I asked Mom.

"In the broth, honey," she said with a tight smile. "For flavor."

"But Mom . . ." My voice broke. "My bet with Lucy . . ."

I tried hard not to cry. I couldn't make a scene right now, not in front of Dad's boss. But I couldn't believe what just happened, either.

I'd eaten beef.

Accident or not, it happened, and I couldn't take it back.

I felt a *whoosh* inside my chest, like how my insides flutter when I'm soaring on the uneven bars and the world blurs around me. But sitting here at the dinner table, I didn't feel that sense of power I felt on the bars. Right now I felt like the world was out of control.

"Oh, Josie, you know how I feel about betting," said Mom, her eyebrows pinching together.

"Don't be so upset, Josie," said Ellen, sweeping away the issue. "It's just a silly bet."

"You don't understand—" My voice cracked again. Sarah looked at me, her eyes wide as if she knew what I was thinking. But she couldn't know—no one at the table did.

I needed that money for my gymnastics registration.

I was already doing the math in my head. Two hundred dollars minus my allowance savings of $76.02 left

$123.98. A lump formed in my throat. Grandma usually slipped twenty dollars in my Christmas card every year, so that left about a hundred dollars my parents would have to cover.

My chin began to tremble. I needed that extra forty dollars. I *needed* it!

Ms. Coburn continued talking as if the beef thing never happened, so I sat through the rest of the dinner silent and without an appetite. I wasn't paying attention at all until I heard Dad say, "*What?*" in a surprised voice. "In my eight years with the company, there's always been a holiday bonus."

"Not this year, Stephen, and for good reason. Our customer service center is being outsourced because the team can't keep up with the demand."

"Apple pie, anyone?" Mom asked, trying to ease the tension in the room. She passed around small plates.

"Me!" cried Amelia.

"Ahh, carbs," said Ms. Coburn, fluttering her fingers a few inches from her mouth. "I'll have to pass, but thank you, Emily."

Dad wasn't ready to give up. "This sends a bad message to the employees."

"I'm sorry, Stephen, but there's nothing I can do.

Upper management met the other day, and—" Suddenly Ms. Coburn screamed and jumped to her feet. "That—that—THING!"

"What thing?" Dad sounded confused. "Josie are you feeding Sugar under the table again?"

I shook my head. Ms. Coburn knocked her chair over. A familiar pink snout appeared from beneath the table. How did she get out of her Cave? Hamlet stood up on her hind legs, her front hooves clunking against the dining room table, flipping the apple pie over onto Ms. Coburn's green sweater.

Oh no!

Hamlet didn't mean to attack her, but it sure looked like she did, that's how badly she wanted apple pie. Sugar barked loudly, and Ms. Coburn tried to swat Hamlet away with her napkin, but Hamlet was a real bully and practically knocked her down on the floor.

"Hamlet's friendly!" I shouted, scrambling to get closer. But in the chaos of the room, I couldn't push past the others. I saw Ms. Coburn raise her leg before it happened. My heartbeat skyrocketed. "Don't! PLEASE!"

Ms. Coburn kicked Hamlet hard, right in the belly, with the toe of her high-heeled boot. And not just once—*twice*. "STOP!" I yelled. Hamlet squealed, and she slowly backed away from her.

"DON'T!" Dad lunged for Hamlet's throat and gently tugged her by the collar, pulling her away from the apple pie mess across Ms. Coburn, her chair, and the floor. Hamlet's snout was covered in pie crust and apple filling, but she calmly stayed right by Dad's side, as if all she had wanted was a little taste and she'd finally come to her senses.

A terrible silence filled the dining room. Ms. Coburn's mouth was open, but no words came out. Dad was out of breath as he gasped out, "No creature, great or small, animal or human, will ever be kicked under this roof. I think it would be best if we ended the night early." Ms. Coburn's jaw dropped. "I'll get your coat."

Mom handed Ms. Coburn a napkin. She brushed apple pie filling off her sweater. I watched as globs of it were flung onto the floor. "Never in my life have I been treated in such an inhospitable fashion," she said, her cheeks turning bright red. "I could sue you over—"

"It's quite obvious that the pig caused no harm besides soiling your sweater," Mom broke in. "We'll pay for the dry cleaning, of course."

"Of course," Dad agreed. He pulled his wallet from his pocket and handed Ms. Coburn two twenty-dollar bills. "That should more than cover it. Now. I'll walk you to the door."

No one dared speak as Ms. Coburn was escorted from the house. I fell to my knees, wrapping my arms around Hamlet's thick neck.

"You okay?" I whispered into the pig's twitching ears. She slobbered my cheek, which was her way of saying that she was just fine. I turned to Mom. "I'm sorry about your pie. I'll clean up the mess."

"Let's do it together," Mom whispered back. She handed us girls some napkins. The front door slammed shut, and Dad reappeared in the doorway. "Stephen?" Mom said. It was a question without even asking one.

Dad ran a hand through his hair. His wedding band caught the light—no. It was the Christmas tree in the living room. Dad had turned Doug's lights back on.

"Dinner was wonderful, Emily," Dad said to my mom. He sounded defeated, but he rubbed her shoulder.

"And your crab cakes were just the right temperature,"

Mom said back, raising a hand and placing it over his.

"C'mon, girls. Let Mom and Dad talk." Ellen retreated to the living room, a book tucked under her arm, and motioned us to follow.

"Can we turn the heat down now?" asked Amelia, wiping her forehead. "I'm sweating!"

"Yeah, we can tell," said Sarah.

I took a deep breath and turned to Dad. "Are you going to get fired?"

"Don't you worry about that, Josie." Dad gave me a halfhearted smile. "Don't you worry about a thing."

His words were something like a switch inside of me, turning off the tears and making me feel stronger. I got to my feet and gave Dad a hug. Even though he's not Hamlet's biggest fan, Dad tried to protect her tonight.

"Thank you," I told him. Dad squeezed me back. He seemed to know what I was thankful for without me even saying it. Suddenly, he burst out laughing. And once he started, he couldn't stop. We all stared at him, confused.

"What's so funny?" Sarah asked.

"Her face! When Hamlet flipped the pie . . ." Dad was laughing so hard he could barely catch a breath.

Mom started chuckling, too. "I've never seen her so disgusted in my entire time with the company. That was great. Just great. Good 'ol Hamlet."

Amelia giggled. I grinned, watching as Dad patted Hamlet on the head. He didn't even pull out the hand sanitizer afterward. Mom watched him for a moment, and then clapped her hands.

"Okay, everyone! Get your coats on. Let's drive around and look at all the holiday lights."

"Really?" I felt my spirits lift. Dad didn't even complain about losing a good parking spot.

"Hooray!" shouted Amelia, flying towards the hall closet.

"I call front seat!" said Sarah, snatching her wool hat off the coat rack and tugging it down on her head.

"What about the dishes?" yelled Ellen from the kitchen.

"We'll deal with them later," said Dad. "But Josie, let's put Hamlet away, just in case." He winked at me, and I reached for her collar, gently tugging her back to her Cave.

Could it be possible?

Maybe Sully was right. Maybe the Three-Week Rule was real . . . and maybe it meant Hamlet was already a part of the Shilling family, and just not everyone had realized it yet.

If I could just stall Dr. Stern and her friends another week or two, then time would tell if Hamlet was staying, or if Hamlet was still going.

Soon I would find out.

Chapter 11

HAMLET'S ESCAPE

Nothing could bother me today.

Not Amelia stealing my favorite T-shirt out of my dresser, or Sarah's remarks about Hamlet stinking up the hallway, or how Ellen ignored me during breakfast, even when I asked her to pass the cereal three times. Because today at school, Sully had a few more good reasons to add to the Case for Keeping Hamlet. Then at practice, I didn't fall off the balance beam once, we got to play in the cheese pit, and I came in *second* in the handstand contest, which never ever happens!

There were just ten days to go before my big meet. All I needed to do was keep my focus—*and* not grow any taller. Too bad I could only control one of those things.

But today? Today I felt like I was walking on clouds, my heart was so light.

Unfortunately I wasn't *actually* walking on clouds—I was cleaning Hamlet's Cave while Amelia and Lou played with Hamlet outside. I gathered up the old ratty towel on the floor to throw in the wash and gave her bag of dried pellet food a shake. It was nearly empty.

No!

How could she be out of food already? Ugh. It was my responsibility to pay for her food—and a bag cost *twenty dollars*. Another purchase was going to make a big dent in my savings, and I needed every penny of my allowance money to go toward my registration fee.

I'd figure that out later. Right now, I needed to finish taking care of Hamlet so I could practice holding splits—three minutes on each side—and do my Language Arts homework. Coach also gave us a lecture about getting to bed at a decent time, which is sometimes hard to do when you share a room with three sisters, but I was determined to make it happen. My body needed the rest now more than ever.

As I crawled out of Hamlet's Cave, I tripped over my little sister's backpack and stubbed my toe. "OW! *Amelia!*" I yelled. She didn't answer, so I craned my neck down the hall. The back door was wide open. "MIL-LIE!"

Ugh! No one in this family ever answers me when I need them.

I stomped to the back door. Amelia and Lou were running around outside in our little yard, and Amelia was trying to get Hamlet to catch a Frisbee in the air.

"Millie!" I scolded. "Why is my pig wearing your old tutu?"

"She's not *your* pig," said Amelia as she hopped around. "Besides! She likes it, see?" I couldn't tell whether Hamlet liked it or not, but she looked absolutely ridiculous with frilly fabric fluttering around her waist. "C'mon, Ham, just like *this*!" Amelia continued, flicking her wrist and releasing the Frisbee. Then she sprinted across the snow and caught it. "Ta-da! Easy."

I held back a grin. Amelia is fast like our brother, but I wasn't about to tell her that. I was too mad about her leaving her stuff around.

"You're throwing it too hard," said Lou, shaking his head. He retrieved the Frisbee and gave it a gentle toss across the yard.

Hamlet just stood there, snout lifted, sniffing the air.

"She's not a dog," I told them. "*Or* a doll to dress up. Okay, piglet playtime is over. I need to get her inside."

But Hamlet had other plans. She dug her hooves into the snow like she was looking for something but couldn't tunnel quite deep enough. I walked over and tried to pick her up, but she wasn't having it. She squealed at the top of her lungs, making my heartbeat thump wildly. Hamlet was too independent for her own good!

"*Shhh!!!*" I scolded her. "You're going to get us in trouble!"

I looked toward Mrs. Taglioni's yard and pressed my tongue against my cheek. Even though I couldn't see through the fence we shared, I knew exactly what was over there, because I'd seen her backyard from my bedroom window for as long as I could remember, and it always looked the same.

Small patch of grass, always cut short in the summer and shoveled clean of snow in the winter.

White iron patio set with a striped canopy, like a photo in a magazine.

"C'mon, Hamlet. It's time for your bath," I said, exhaling my frustration. I didn't have time for this!

I picked her up, gripping her legs as hard as I could. Her hooves kicked at my arms, and she squealed. "Hammie—shhh!" I scolded her. She tried to jump out of my arms as I walked up the patio steps, and the tutu wriggled right off her back.

"Hey! You're getting my tutu dirty!"

"It shouldn't have been on her in the first place."

I tried to open the door, but Hamlet still had other plans. She oinked and grunted and twisted until finally she was *so* loud and squirmy and her hooves were digging grooves into my sweater that I had no choice but to set her down.

Great. Now I'd have to chase her inside the house, and it was freezing out. I stuck my hands in my pockets, trying to warm them up.

"She doesn't want to go inside yet," said Lou.

"Obviously." I narrowed my eyes at him and moved toward the pig again. She bolted out of my grasp each time I approached her. She was quick! "Anyway. It's getting dark out. Hamlet needs a bath and dinner, and I have homework to do and routines to practice. Millie, I told you that Hamlet has to be on a leash . . . *Now* look at her!"

"Pigs shouldn't wear leashes," Amelia said. "Right, Lou?"

"Well." He wrinkled his face as if he wanted to ask his mom about it before having an opinion on the matter.

"*Not* right, Millie." I put my hands on my hips. "Maybe farm pigs don't wear leashes, but city pigs do, okay? It's for safety. I'm sure Lou's mom would agree with me on that! Now. Help me get Hamlet inside."

But every time we stepped closer to Hamlet, she moved further away from us. Hmm. This tactic wasn't working. "We need snacks," I told the kids. "Millie, Lou, go grab crackers so we can lead her in, okay?"

Amelia and Lou raced up the back steps and into the house. A brisk wind swept across the yard, sending a shiver across my bare arms. I should've told them to grab my coat, too. The last thing I needed was to get sick so close to my meet.

"C'mon, Hamlet," I tried again, frustration brewing inside of me. I took another step toward her, nearly grabbing her hind legs. But she galloped right past me and squeezed underneath our snow-covered picnic table.

"HAMLET! Ugh!"

But I wasn't giving up on her. Not with the snowstorm rolling in tonight and Hamlet's warm bath waiting for her inside. She was only a piglet and I knew what was best for her, even if she didn't want to listen to me.

"Now. Let's *go*!"

I stretched out my arms.

She scooted out of the way.

I lunged. "Aha, I've got ya!" I cried, grabbing her torso. But her back was covered with snow, and just like that, Hamlet slipped from my grasp. She jumped up on the picnic table and broke through the fence, leaping right into Mrs. Taglioni's yard!

It took everything in my body not to scream.

"Um, what just happened?" said a small voice behind me.

I stared in disbelief at the broken fence. I couldn't think about that now. I couldn't answer Amelia now. I had to go where I'd never been before—Mrs. Taglioni's yard—and get that pig back like my life depended on it.

The kids were on my heels. I yelled for them to stay back. They'd only make things worse.

"Don't!" cried Amelia. "You *can't*!"

I didn't have a choice. I hopped up on the picnic table and scaled the fence into Mrs. Taglioni's yard just like Hamlet had done moments before. I landed on a soft bed of snow, and my heart sunk. There was debris all around me: plants wrapped in plastic bags to keep the frost away were toppled over, their ceramic

132

pots shattered. Hamlet had been here—and had made a huge mess.

I spotted muddy hoofprints in the snow and followed them until I laid eyes on my piglet. She turned her head, ears twitching. We locked eyes.

"Hamlet," I begged. "Please just *stay* there!"

Hamlet was a flash of pink—a little lightning bolt zipping across the yard, looking for a way out. I pumped my arms and chased her up and down the fence line, pleading for her not to break through another wooden plank.

I'd give her belly rubs, if she just listened to me.

Make corn on the cob—her favorite!

Take her on an extra-long walk tomorrow, even though I didn't have time.

Please, please, please.

But Hamlet didn't listen. She galloped right up the back steps of Mrs. Taglioni's house and then disappeared from sight.

Ugh! Where did she go?

I tiptoed up the steps. Maybe Mrs. Taglioni wasn't home. Maybe I could still get out of here alive.

"Hamlet!" I whispered, searching for her. "Hammieeee!"

But then my eyes fell on it: the small, plastic doggie flap at the base of Mrs. Taglioni's back door. I'd forgotten about how she had it custom-made for her cats last summer, so they could be outdoor and indoor cats, and that she'd told us to not leave food in the backyard, because she didn't trust that Sugar would leave them alone if they jumped the fence.

Like Sugar even cared about her cats.

I knelt to the ground. Maybe the little door was locked, so cold air and snow didn't come inside. I gave it a gentle push. The door was cold to the touch, but it flapped frontward and backward.

A terrifying scream reached my ears, followed by a high-pitched piglet squeal that I'd recognize anywhere.

Hamlet!

I had no choice.

I knocked on the door.

Mrs. Taglioni's door flew open and slammed closed behind her. She stared at me, wild-eyed.

"There's. A. Pig. In. My. House!" she cried, placing a palm over her heart.

I couldn't even imagine how much trouble I'd be in after my parents heard about this. I'd be lucky if I ever did a cartwheel again.

"About that . . ." I crossed my arms, trying to keep away the cold, and pretended that I had Tom's confidence. Maybe I could calm Mrs. Taglioni down. There was a chance, even if it was a *small* one. "So . . . um. Remember that puppy we're pet sitting? Yeah. Not a puppy. But she's friendly, I promise!"

"Are you telling me that's a *Shilling* pig?"

Her words weren't flames, but her angry tone burned me inside all the same. All the confidence inside me turned to ash. I nodded and tried not to cry. Then Mrs. Taglioni did something that I wasn't expecting. She went back inside the house, leaving me standing on the doorstep.

"Um? Hello?" I called in through the screen door. "HELLO?"

I suddenly caught a whiff of a thick, sweet aroma floating out of the townhouse, something I hadn't noticed in the yard before. Mrs. Taglioni opened the screen door, and Hamlet came barreling out. Good thing I was quick enough to reach down and grab her before she bolted back into the yard.

"If it weren't for my cats, my homemade corn chowder would be on the floor right now in a shattered crockpot," Mrs. Taglioni yelled, narrowing her eyes.

I drew Hamlet closer to my chest. She was a *very! bad! piglet!* but her body trembled and her heart raced. I stroked her across her back, trying to calm her down. "Did they hurt her?" I asked.

"They chased her away," Mrs. Taglioni snapped, fire in her voice. "And rightfully so! If I ever see that pig around here again, I'll—"

Mrs. Taglioni's jaw dropped open. She was staring off at something behind me, something so unbelievably horrible that even she couldn't find the words, which was like a *first* for Mrs. Taglioni.

I didn't need to turn around.

I already knew the damage that Hamlet had done.

Mrs. Taglioni rolled her shoulders back and said the worst four words I'd ever heard her say in my whole life.

"I'm. Calling. Your. Mother."

Chapter 12

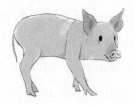

DOWN FOR THE COUNT

Please don't say I'm grounded, I begged Mom with my eyes. *Please, please, please.*

Mom's lips drew into a thin line. She had barely said a word since I got home. I'd only received instructions with clipped words. *Josie, clean Hamlet's litter box. Finish your homework. Then find me—we need to have a talk.*

I'd done as she asked, but it was hard to calm the nerves fluttering in my stomach. I didn't know exactly what Mrs. Taglioni told her, but I knew that *both* of them were upset with me.

I rubbed baby shampoo all over Hamlet's body until she was covered in bubbles. She tried to slurp up the bathwater, and I lifted her snout away. She knew just how to make me laugh, even when I was feeling my lowest.

"Hammie!" I scooped up water and rinsed her back. The pig turned toward me and snorted hard through her big round nostrils, blowing a stream of bubbles in my face. I giggled. "You're lucky you're this cute," I told her, rinsing the rest of her body off.

As I drained the bathwater, I towel-dried her off and then lifted her out onto the bath mat. She was so heavy! Come springtime—if I was allowed to keep her that long, and things weren't looking promising—I'd have to bathe her with the garden hose out back.

After I tucked Hamlet into her Cave, I made a snack of celery sticks with ranch dressing and flopped open my Science book to the new lesson. It was usually my best subject, but I couldn't focus, not tonight. It took me twice as long to finish the questions at the end of the section.

While I waited for Mom to finish helping Amelia with her homework, I closed my eyes and visualized my balance beam routine, but even then, Hamlet invaded my thoughts. I imagined the piglet bolting across the gym and jumping over the beam right when I was attempting a back walkover, making me fall off onto the mat.

I opened my eyes.

I just needed to get the conversation over with.

I found Mom wearing her fuzzy bathrobe and brewing hot tea in the kitchen. "Want a cup?" she asked, looking up, and I shook my head. She glanced out the window into the dark backyard and I felt my nerves flare up again. "Let's go sit on the couch," she finally said.

Once we took our seats, I blurted, "What did Mrs. Taglioni tell you?"

Mom dunked a tea bag in the mug, carefully choosing her words. "That Hamlet jumped into her yard, knocking over some fencing and planters. She mentioned that the pig ran into her house, too, Josie. You can imagine she was very upset about all of this. . . ."

I swallowed hard. "Yeah, she wasn't too happy."

My mom sighed. "You'll have to pay for the damage, Josie."

"No way." I sat upright. "It wasn't my fault, Mom! It was—"

"Hamlet's fault," she finished. "I know it feels that way, Josie. But you agreed to take responsibility for her and that means actions have consequences. We can't leave that fence broken. It's a safety hazard, not to mention our property line with Mrs. Taglioni. You should have heard how angry she was over her broken planters.

She said the total damage could be four hundred dollars—maybe more! Do you realize how much money that is? And with the van just getting fixed, and the holidays coming up, this is all terrible timing. . . ."

"But I told Amelia to put Hamlet on a leash."

"You're the big sister. If Millie didn't listen to you, you could have put Hamlet on the leash yourself. Now." She took a deep breath. "When your father and I gave you permission to keep the pig until New Year's, you agreed that you'd be responsible for Hamlet's actions. I know you won't be happy to hear this, Josie, but I expect you to pay for some of the damage with your saved allowance money. And for the next month, there will be no more weekly allowance."

My eyes welled up with tears. Paying for the fence was a ton better than getting grounded and missing my gymnastics meet this weekend, but still. The last thing I wanted to do was use my precious allowance money on boring things like fencing and planters.

I did a quick calculation. I had $76.02 in savings. And Hamlet was almost out of food, so I needed twenty dollars to cover that. If the destruction bills totaled four hundred dollars, my parents would still have to pay $343.98 to cover the rest of the damages.

$343.98.

There's no way my parents would pay the two hundred dollar gymnastics fee on top of that.

What that meant was absolutely devastating.

I'd lose my spot on the team.

I began to sob uncontrollably. Mom rubbed my back and said, "Oh, sweetie, I know you're hurting inside right now. This just gives me more reassurance that Hamlet would be happier living at a farm, Josie. She's a sweet little pig, but she's not meant for city life."

"Hamlet was hungry. She just smelled the corn chowder is all." I stared into Doug's flickering Christmas lights, but through the tears it felt like I was swimming in a sea of blurry red and green waves. I couldn't even think about Hamlet being taken away from me on top of losing my allowance money *and* my gymnastics spot. It was too much.

Sugar trotted over and nestled her gray snout against my knee. I patted her head and she lay down beside the couch. Even though I was furious with Hamlet, I wished I could let her out of the Cave to snuggle with her, too. Animals just had a way of making me feel better.

"And there's something else," Mom started, her eyebrows pinching together.

I looked up in alarm. "What?"

"Lou's mom called me today. She said she'd been trying to reach us all week?"

I leaned against the couch cushion. This night couldn't get any worse.

"Well, I'm afraid I have bad news. . . . She had friends interested in adopting Hamlet. They sounded like a wonderful family, too. But when Dr. Stern asked about her current temperament and if she'd ever shown aggression, well . . ." Mom cleared her throat. "I had to tell her about what happened with Ms. Coburn. It was the right thing to do."

"Oh, Mom!" I said. I didn't want to send Hamlet away, but I also didn't want anyone thinking badly of her. She was the sweetest pig I knew. "Hamlet only wanted the pie, she would never hurt anyone! She's just a hungry pig going through a growth spurt, that's all!"

"I know, sweetie. But it's the truth, all the same. I wouldn't feel comfortable if we didn't disclose all the details in advance." Mom sipped her hot tea. "Well, let's just say that they've decided that Hamlet sounds more wild creature than pet, and they've decided to pass. I believe they were concerned with *aggressive dominant and feral behavior.*"

Hamlet wasn't aggressive or dominant. I wasn't quite sure what feral meant, but I was pretty positive she wasn't that, either.

"Have you been working to find her a home, honey?" Mom asked after a long pause.

I drew in a deep, shaky breath instead of answering her. I was still hoping the Case for Keeping Hamlet was wide open. I couldn't imagine giving her away. Just the thought of it made my heart ache inside.

"You promised us that you'd find Hamlet a family, Josie," Mom reminded me gently. "And you need to keep that promise."

Why couldn't my mom see how important Hamlet was to me? That I needed her in my life?

Words didn't come. Instead, I clutched the fabric of my long-sleeved pajama shirt and wiped away my tears.

"Now." Mom tucked a lock of hair behind my ear but her voice was firm. "About the fence. I know this is hard for you, Josie, and I'm sorry for that. It's hard for me, too. But you need to pay for the damage that Hamlet caused. I'll discuss it with your father when he comes home from work tonight, but I know that he'll agree."

Paying for the damage meant the end of my allowance

savings. Months of not buying things I wanted to buy because gymnastics meant more to me. It felt like my heart was going to burst. But instead, the tears burst instead, streaming down my cheeks.

I didn't have a choice.

"I'm sorry, Mom," I said. Her face crumpled up, and she leaned in to give me a hug.

"I'm sorry, too, sweetie. I know this is hard for you. We love you so much."

The front door opened right then, and Dad walked in, stomping the snow off his boots. He pulled off his coat and wool hat, hanging them on the back of the door, before spotting us.

"We're in here," Mom called out. "How was work?"

"Work." Dad sighed a deep, sad sigh, and then said, "I missed four calls from Mrs. Taglioni. She didn't leave a voice mail. Anyone know what that's about?"

Mom and I exchanged a look. Tears overflowed from my eyes all over again, and I crumpled against her chest.

"What?" Dad's eyebrows lifted in alarm. "What's wrong?"

Mom patted my knee. "Go on, Josie."

Dad sat next to me on the couch. I told him through the tears about Hamlet busting the fence and bolting into Mrs. Taglioni's house and how much the damages might cost. I watched as the news sunk in, and his face fell into his hands.

"Dad?" I asked him. "Dad, I'm sorry—I tried—I tried—"

He didn't say anything for a moment. Finally, he reached over and gave my hand a squeeze so I knew he wasn't mad at me, but still, he wouldn't look me in the eyes.

We sat in silence for a minute, just listening to the faint *whoosh* of car tires slushing through the snow on the busy street outside. I exhaled slowly and got off the couch. "Be right back."

I walked down the hall and ignored my parents' whispering behind me. All I heard was Mom ask, "*Did you pay the credit card bill this month?*"

Hamlet was sleeping in her Cave, curled up against an old tattered yellow towel. Her eyes were closed and she rested her snout between her front hooves. She seemed exhausted like she'd fallen into one of those deep sleeps that Sugar has after she goes to the dog park in the summertime. I reached over and patted the top of Hamlet's head. She cracked open one eye in alarm, but when she saw me she closed it right back, that's

145

how much we trusted each other.

"Oh, Hamlet," I said. "What a day." I wasn't even mad at her anymore. It wasn't her fault, not really, and the cats had really scared her. "Good night," I whispered.

Upstairs, in the girls' bedroom, Ellen was reading on the top bed of the bunk she shared with Sarah. Amelia was fast asleep already, and Sarah was listening to music on her headphones. Ellen barely glanced up from her book, but she must've heard me sniffling because she snapped the fantasy book closed and said, "What's wrong with you?"

I squeezed underneath the bunk bed, grabbing my money jar from its hiding place. The glass felt cool on my fingertips.

"Everything," I said, spinning the jar around, listening to the coins and bills rattle inside for the last time. "Just everything."

I tried to squelch the frustration and disappointment tornadoing inside me. I should be working on my mental game, like Coach suggested. I used to spend my evenings memorizing my new routines, watching YouTube videos of the skills at the library, and doing crunches and squats and sun salutations. Now I was too busy feeding Hamlet dinner, giving her baths, walking her in the yard, and cleaning the Cave to do much else besides homework.

It wasn't that I didn't love Hamlet.

I did.

It's just taking care of a piglet was a lot harder than I'd thought it'd be. In saving Hamlet's life, I felt like I was losing some of my own.

Chapter 13

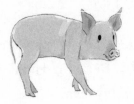

DESPERATE TIMES, DESPERATE MEASURES

Sully's Three-Week Rule is bogus.

I did the math. Hamlet arrived three weeks ago today. Sure, Dad let her sleep with his favorite slippers on Tree Day and even protected her from the wrath of Ms. Coburn last weekend, but then Hamlet damaged the fence and . . . well.

With seventeen days left before New Year's Day, it looked like the Case for Keeping Hamlet was now Case Closed.

How did I know? Because before school at breakfast that morning, Hamlet barreled over the baby gate blocking her Cave and galloped down the hallway. She leapt over Millie's boots in the hall and bullied herself right up against my legs, trying to steal my Pop-Tart.

"Hamlet—no!" I scolded her, looping my fingers around her collar. Then, more calmly because Dad was watching, "Now, Hamlet. You're trying to tell me you need breakfast, aren't you? I'll go feed you now. And don't worry, I scheduled *plenty of time* for a *nice long walk* before school today—"

Before I could lead her back down the hall, Dad wagged his finger at me. "Josie Shilling, wait one moment." I stopped in my tracks. "Time is ticking. That pig has tripled in size since she got here. You need to find Hamlet a home ASAP or I'm going to ship her to anyone in this country that'll take her, for pork or a pet!"

His tone was like a bolt of lightning to my spine, making me stand up straight. "You don't mean it!" I said, tugging her a little closer.

No. He *couldn't* mean it. Could he?

"You need to be picking up the phone and making calls, *today*. That was the agreement *weeks* ago."

"Um, Dad," I said, clearing my throat. "Did Millie tell you how Hamlet learned to catch a Frisbee?"

"Yeah, Dad!" Amelia looked up from her cereal bowl. "It only took like ten times. She's *super* smart. And she can jump really high!"

I grinned. Another reason for keeping Hamlet!

Ellen glanced up from reading the morning newspaper. She had a neighborhood paper route and she always made it a point to read the daily paper to catch up on the news. "Another storm is coming this weekend," she said, tapping the big map of the Midwest on the back page. The entire state of Ohio was colored blue and white. "I hear it's going to be a long, snowy winter."

Dad closed his eyes, massaging his temples in teeny tiny circles. Finally, he took a swig of coffee and reached for his bus card. "I'll be home for dinner. Love you, girls." He leaned down and gave me a kiss on the head. Then he pointed at Hamlet. "But I mean it about Hamlet. Two weeks. And secure that baby gate, okay?"

I nodded and watched Dad head out the door to work, tucking his chin into his coat and trekking through the snow outside. The morning sky was thick and gray, with that looming darkness that's typical of December, when the sun doesn't rise until eight.

If it weren't for the taxicab headlights from the street catching my attention, I never would've noticed what was happening next door at Mrs. Taglioni's house. I squinted my eyes through the bay window. Dr. Stern stood on our neighbor's front stoop, her stethoscope slung around her neck.

The *last* thing I wanted was to get caught up in a conversation with Mrs. Taglioni, but I needed to talk to Dr. Stern and desperate times call for desperate measures.

If the Case for Keeping Hamlet was closed—and I really hoped it wasn't—I needed to find someone who would love her and take good care of her, or Dad was going to make good on his word. If anyone could help me find Hamlet a forever home, it'd be Dr. Stern.

I grabbed my puffy coat, zipped it up, and yelled to my sisters, "Just going next door real quick!" before disappearing into the soft, falling snow. My boots crunched down the steps as I made my way to Mrs. Taglioni's.

"Dr. Stern!" I called out in the howling wind. "You know how you talked to my mom the other day? Maybe you can help—"

"Not now, Josie."

I stopped talking midsentence. I'd been so focused on what I needed to say that I didn't even notice what I *should* be seeing.

Mrs. Taglioni stood at the cracked-open door. Her face was barely visible, but from what I could see, I knew that the *almost impossible* was happening right now, in front of me, on her very front stoop.

She was bawling her eyes out.

Mrs. Taglioni.

Had. A. Heart.

I could barely believe it!

"Mrs. Taglioni?" I said, walking up her stoop steps. "Are you okay?"

Which made her cry even harder. "My poor Ralphie," she sobbed. "He didn't listen to me. Chewed an electrical cord . . . And . . . And . . . it just ZINGED him!"

My gaze dropped to the dark bag in Dr. Stern's hand. "Ralphie . . . ?"

Mrs. Taglioni wiped away her tears with a handkerchief, unable to answer me. Dr. Stern drew the bag closer to her chest and said calmly, "A sugar glider."

"Oh, Mrs. Taglioni," I said, feeling my lower lip start to quiver in sympathy. "I'm so sorry."

She nodded like she heard me, but said nothing in reply. Dr. Stern cleared her throat. "You gave him a good life, Molly," the veterinarian said gently. "He was lucky to have you care for him all these years. If you need to reach me later, you have my number. I'm sorry for your loss."

Mrs. Taglioni nodded again as she pulled the door

closed. Dr. Stern and I turned around and faced the city together. My cheeks tingled from the cold. Cars whizzed by and people stomped down the snow-layered sidewalk, not even taking notice of us or what had just happened.

I felt terrible.

"Now what is it you wanted to talk to me about, Josie?" asked Dr. Stern. "I only have a moment before I need to get Lou on the bus and open the clinic."

"Hamlet . . . I . . . I don't think my parents are going to let me keep her."

"No. Probably not." Dr. Stern tightened her scarf around her neck while balancing her hold on the black bag. I wondered if Mrs. Taglioni was going to bury Ralphie in her backyard and if there were other dead animals back there, too.

"I can't let anything bad happen to her," I said, my voice rising. "I can't!"

Dr. Stern stared me down for a minute. I shifted my weight from my toes to my heels, barely able to wait for her answer.

She *had* to help me.

Hamlet's life depended on it!

"You like animals a lot, don't you, Josie?" Dr. Stern asked finally.

I nodded. "Yeah."

"I was impressed with the way you comforted your pig during her exam and how you've encouraged Hamlet and Sugar to get along. Lou told me that you give Hamlet lots of regular walks and baths, too. I'm happy to hear how well you've cared for her."

"Really? Thanks."

Finally *somebody* noticed how responsible I was being!

"You have a way with animals, Josie. Has anyone told you that before?"

"Um . . . I don't think so," I said.

I felt my cheeks warm. It was the first time in a long time that anyone had complimented me on something I was good at besides gymnastics. I didn't know I *could* be good at anything besides gymnastics.

"Tell you what," Dr. Stern began. "Lou is helping me clean the clinic this evening after the last appointment. Why don't you and Amelia come by around six thirty? You could bring Hamlet, too, if you'd like."

I thought about it for a second. Mom didn't work

today so she had carpool duty, and she was bringing Lucy and me back from gymnastics after school. On Thursdays, we had a quick dinner of sandwiches with just Amelia, since Ellen and Sarah usually studied with friends until later.

"Can Lucy come, too?" I asked. I'd been so busy with Hamlet that I hadn't seen much of my best friend outside of gymnastics lately. I needed her advice now more than ever.

"Of course," said Dr. Stern. "We can talk about Hamlet's situation then. I'm not sure I'll be able to help you, Josie, so don't get your hopes up, but I'll certainly try. How does that sound?"

"Sounds great!" I exclaimed, but then immediately felt bad for being so happy right here on Mrs. Taglioni's stoop, just minutes after she'd shed tears in this very spot.

"Great, see you later. Have a good day at school," Dr. Stern said. Her gloved hand tightened the grip on the black bag and she disappeared down the block toward her clinic.

I turned around and stared at the door of Mrs. Taglioni's little townhouse. All the curtains and blinds were closed. Her heart must be hurting so bad right now. She was probably curled up in bed with her favorite blanket and a cat or two.

Maybe Mrs. Taglioni and I weren't so different after all, I realized. We wanted the best things for our pets and couldn't always get what we wished for, no matter how badly we tried.

Chapter 14

STICKS AND STONES

The blisters on my palms broke in Physical Education class.

One of them started pussing and even bleeding a little bit, so I had to go to the nurse's office to get cleaned up. By next period, Fernanda had heard the rumor that I was sick and rushed to sit next to me in Math, the one class we shared together.

"I thought you got sent home!" she said, and then noticed the gauze around my right hand. "Oh no— What happened?!"

I felt my face redden. Other kids were looking at me, too, and the last thing I wanted was their attention. "Nothing," I told her. "Just normal rips from gymnastics. Been working hard on my bar routine lately."

"Ohhhh. Okay." That seemed to satisfy her concern, since Fernanda pulled her ratios homework from her backpack and said cheerfully, "How's Hamlet?"

"Adorable and causing mischief, as usual." I sighed.

Mr. Willis called our attention to the front of the room. "Homework, please! Pass it up to the front row," he called out, and I felt my face flush again. Everything in my life had been so messy lately, it had totally slipped my mind.

Fernanda wiggled her fingers over her shoulder. When no paper touched her hand, she turned her head. "Josie?"

"Forgot," I admitted. Fernanda's eyes narrowed in concern—I never forgot to do my homework—but she didn't say anything.

As Mr. Willis started in on his lecture, I pulled the white gauze off my hand. The bleeding had stopped, and the nurse was just trying to protect the skin. But she couldn't—that's not how it worked. I needed my hands, even if they were injured ones.

I sighed, zoning out, staring at my palms where the skin was raw. Gymnasts called them *rips*. They were the worst I'd had in probably . . . forever. Usually rips didn't hurt too bad, just stung a little, but this time, the pain was more sharp and obvious.

After school at gymnastics practice, each time I chalked up my too-tight, worn grips, I felt dust cake against my open wounds. When I reached my arms high above my head, elbows pinched against my ears, it took at least five swings to mentally block out the burn searing across my palms.

Still, too tight or not, Lucy's old grips were in better shape than my ratty ones, and I had to make do. Our big Level 5 meet was in three days and I couldn't lose my focus now, no matter how many problems bounced around in my head.

No. I wasn't going to let blisters or pigs or dead sugar gliders or empty allowance jars or *anything* get in the way of my focus. I'd worked too hard for this, and I wasn't going to let my team—or myself—down now.

At gymnastics practice, Coach was in full-on competition mode, not cutting any of us a break. She expected *perfection*.

"Wrap it up, girls! Toes UP! Squeeeeeeze those abdominals! Toes UP! Toes to BAR!"

We finished our uneven bar conditioning and Coach waved us over to the vault. My stomach quivered as I lined up behind Lucy. I could see the springboard from over her head. I squeezed my eyes shut, remembering Tom's advice.

We've all got something to bring to the team.

Tom's advice helped me before. But my nerves felt electric today, like when a storm is brewing and you'd better take cover before it hits.

I knew this storm.

It was fear.

"Can't believe we have only two more practices left before the meet," Lucy whispered over her shoulder as warm-up passes began. "Oh—your braid is falling out." She quickly fixed it and tightened my ponytail holder.

"Thanks," I said.

Maxie took her turn. *Sprint, sprint, POUND!*

Butterflies danced in my stomach. "Me either."

Becky bolted ahead of us and punched her feet onto the springboard, raising her arms over her head as she soared, tight and long, landing solidly on her feet. We all did the same and looped back to the line. Coach always says warm-ups have to do with muscle memory. Like, your body can be trained to remember certain movements, but you have to remind it first. Each time we switch gears and start a new apparatus, we do a few practice pass-throughs with really basic skills, just to trigger those muscle memories.

"Still on for the clinic after practice?" Lucy asked me while we waited to take our turns.

"Yep." I pressed up on my toes. "I've been meaning to tell you something . . ."

"What's that?"

"I ate beef. In a soup." I leaned back onto my heels. "It was an accident, but I guess that means I lost the bet."

"Oh." Lucy smiled. "I forgot to tell you I lost the bet, too. We had chicken fajitas last weekend. I couldn't help myself!"

We stared at each other, a moment of silence hovering in the air, and then both busted out laughing. Coach clapped her hands loudly—*one, two!*—across the room and I groaned.

"Vault time."

Lucy adjusted her leotard and shot me a grin. "Oh, Josie. Such a worrywart! You've got your handspring down! I'm the one who doesn't get enough height on it."

My gaze shifted back to the gymnastics apparatus. "Yeah. I've got the height part down," I muttered.

Maybe warm-ups are supposed to help my body,

but sometimes they just mess with my brain. When we're moving at a slower pace, I have time to catch my reflection in the mirrors on the other side of the gym. It makes me round my shoulders and then Coach calls me out on my bad posture. Or when we're waiting in line, I start to overthink the new skills in the routines, and all of a sudden I'm afraid I'm going to fail and let everyone down or get an injury or . . .

I drew in a sharp breath to block out the distractions. Maxie finished her turn, a few girls ahead of me. Lucy went next, and her vault was solid, even though her legs split a little and her normally pointed toes were a little sloppy.

When it was my turn, I pretended that I was a pouncing tiger in the brush, imagining how high I could spring, how perfect and graceful my form could be. *My angles will be spot on*, I told myself. *My hands will power off the vault, but not pause. It'll be a handspring over the vault table like Coach has never seen before.*

"Make it happen, Josie! Tight, tight, tight!" coach yelled from down the line. I practiced saluting the invisible judges. "Quick feet, quick feet! Pump those arms and POUND!"

I sprinted and punched the springboard hard with my

feet, stretching up, as tall and tight as I can be. I flipped forward over the vault, palms pressing down quick on the top. I felt my body whip forward as I over-rotated and flipped, landing on my feet but falling backward and *smack!* right down on my bottom.

I met Coach's eyes. She pinched her lips together. "Watch your control. Shake those nerves next time. You're rotating too quickly. Mind over matter."

"Mind over matter. Right." Coach could probably hear my heartbeat pounding as I got to my feet and dusted off my hands.

I moved from the mat and started back to my team's line. Mandy, a Level 10 gymnast who always wore neon-colored practice leotards and had the prettiest curly brown hair, stood alongside a balance beam, chalking up her feet. She smirked when our eyes made contact.

"Not bad, Josie Long Legs," she muttered, just loud enough for me to hear.

Josie Long Legs?

Heat rushed my cheeks. I lowered my eyes, not sure what to say. The older girls had nicknames for us . . . and mine was *Josie Long Legs*?

Even though the cool winter air blew into the

gymnastics center from the cracked-open windows, my body felt like it was on fire.

Josie Long Legs.

It confirmed my fears that everyone saw how tall I was, how wrong I was built for this sport of teeny tiny, super-strong girls.

I jogged back to the team and stood behind Lucy. She was so much shorter than me, the perfect size for a gymnast. "You can do this vault no problem," she encouraged me before our second pass.

"So can you!" I said, meaning every word.

My best friend patted me on the shoulder. Instead of making me feel better, it just reminded me of how tall I was growing, and that I couldn't stop it from happening. To the Level 10 girls, Lucy probably looked like a perfectly petite fairy comforting an awkward gangly giant.

I wished I could pull my legs into my body like a turtle hides in its shell.

Chapter 15

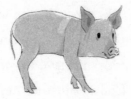

JUST WHAT THE DOCTOR ORDERED

After gymnastics, Mom made turkey sandwiches and Lucy and I walked over to Dr. Stern's clinic with Amelia. Even though the sky is already dark by 6:00 p.m. in the wintertime, there are so many streetlights that Mom told us Hamlet could only come if we carried her so the neighbors didn't see.

We hid Hamlet inside my gymnastics bag, zipping it closed just enough so her head could poke out for fresh air. "Awww, poor Hammie wants to *walk*!" protested Amelia, pointing to the way the pig lifted her snout into the air, catching a scent.

Amelia held up the leash triumphantly. "Brought this!" she said, and I shook my head. I wasn't risking Hamlet getting loose in our neighborhood or getting in trouble with my parents. Hamlet met my eyes and squealed in protest, trying to wiggle out of the bag.

It felt like my heart twisted inside just thinking about poor Hamlet not being able to run around. "She's not allowed to walk through the neighborhood," I reminded them with a sigh. "Mom's orders."

"But your mom doesn't have to carry her! She's. So. HEAVY!" huffed Lucy, adjusting her grip on the bag. My palms felt like they were on fire, and finally we had to set Hamlet down for a second to take a break in front of the library. "We should make the team carry Hamlet and run sprints," said Lucy, giggling. "It'd make conditioning more fun at least."

"Oh no, my bag's getting wet!" I pointed at the snow. Hamlet tried to wriggle out of the bag, but I petted her head and commanded, "STAY, Hamlet," and she nestled down into her yellow towel.

Ugh. I'd have to scrub my gym bag now.

It was only a few blocks to the veterinary clinic, but when you're carrying a heavy piglet it feels like a marathon. We walked up to the first-floor unit of Lou's townhouse, where Dr. Stern's business was. Lou was waiting for us, wiping down the big entryway mirrors.

"Hey, guys!" he said, and Amelia ran up next to him

and started going through his box of cleaning supplies. Lucy and I set my gym bag down in the lobby, making sure the front door was closed behind us, and I lifted Hamlet out of the bag.

The pig immediately pressed her snout to the floor tiles, sniffing everything from the magazine rack to the bags of dog food for sale to the stack of this morning's issue of *City Centennial*. Finally, she looped back around and slobbered Lucy's hand.

"Hammie!" Lucy squealed. Hamlet oinked and wiggled in response. "You are one big pig."

"She knocked me over the other day," Amelia said. The mirror squeaked as she rubbed it down with a white rag.

"Not really a piglet anymore, are you, Hamlet," I said, giving her a big pat on the back.

"Josie!" Dr. Stern appeared from down the long hall. "Perfect timing. And hiya, Lucy. And look what we have here!" She bent down to pet Hamlet. The pig jumped up on her lap, and the vet laughed, gently pushing her hooves back down to the tiles. "Look how big she is!" Then she waved to Lucy and me. "I'm just starting the afternoon rounds with my patients. You girls want to join me?"

"Sure!" I said.

"Amelia, Lou, mirrors are looking good!"

Lou grinned, revealing a gap between his front teeth. "Mirrors are my specialty," said Amelia. I laughed at how much she sounded like Tom sometimes. Amelia complained every time we had to pick up our room, but here at the veterinarian clinic, cleaning was like recess for her.

"What about glass?" said Dr. Stern, smiling. "Windows are next."

"Glass, too!"

"Can Hamlet be loose to explore?" I asked Dr. Stern.

She nodded. "As long as the front door is closed. Lou, Amelia, help keep an eye on Hamlet, will you?"

"Yeah—a *close* eye," I emphasized, remembering the backyard escape.

Dr. Stern gave the younger kids the thumbs-up and motioned my best friend and me to the kennels, which were in the back part of the clinic. The first patient was a speckled cat that was practically as big as Hamlet.

"Meet Atticus." Dr. Stern tapped a chart that dangled from a clipboard on the wall. "Adopted recently and just had surgery. We kept him overnight for observation. Eyes are clear. Looks like he's drinking water and eating." Atticus stretched his paws out and yawned.

"He doesn't have claws," Lucy observed.

"Correct. He was declawed, probably many years ago by the previous owner," said Dr. Stern. "Atticus was found eating out of a Dumpster a few miles from here, and animal control picked him up. When no one claimed him, a new family adopted him. Atticus is well into his senior years now. How are you feeling this morning, Atticus?"

The big cat pressed his body against the cage, and Dr. Stern squeezed her fingers through the metal bars to pet his soft fur. Atticus let out a deep, throaty purr, making us all laugh. "Seems to be doing just fine," Dr. Stern said with a grin. "His new family will be picking him up in an hour. Onto the next patient . . . "

The cage above Atticus appeared to be empty. I stood on my tiptoes to get a better look inside. Dr. Stern tapped gently on the bars, and an itty-bitty black puppy pressed its wet nose against the cage. It started whining as soon as it saw us, and Dr. Stern unhooked and opened the door, taking the puppy into her arms.

"It's so adorable!" I gasped. "Can I pet it?"

"Me, too!" said Lucy.

"Sure. This is Oliver. He's a black Lab, about nine weeks old."

The puppy was the cutest thing I'd ever seen—besides when Hamlet was a little pink piglet, of course. Everything about Oliver was so tiny and innocent. Dr. Stern handed him to me, and I cradled his furry, warm body in my arms.

"Aww . . . I remember when Hamlet was this tiny!" I said. Oliver stretched up and licked my chin, slobbering me.

Lucy laughed, but then the smile vanished from her face. "Oh no—What's wrong with Oliver? Is he sick?"

"Perfect health." Dr. Stern tapped his chart. "I'm just keeping a close eye on him while his owners are away for the holidays. Josie, would you like to hold Oliver while Lucy and I check on one last patient?"

The puppy wriggled up against my chest, as if he liked hearing my heartbeat and feeling the warmth of my wool sweater. "Sure!"

"Okay. Hold him tight, he's a wiggler."

"Trust me," I said, thinking of all the times I'd held Hamlet. "I know all about wigglers!"

We shadowed Dr. Stern as she moved to a glass aquarium, peeking in on a green iguana that had suffered a tail injury. Dr. Stern had amputated the iguana's tail and it was all bandaged up. Then we put Oliver back in his kennel and did a final walk-through of the clinic. We helped empty all the garbage cans in the examination rooms while Dr. Stern gave the animals fresh water and food.

"Wow, I wish I had you girls to help me all the time!" Dr. Stern said with a wink. "Who needs a part-time job?"

I laughed, pulling warm, clean towels from the dryer. As I folded them, I realized my heart wasn't racing and my skin wasn't electric with nerves and I was even *humming* to myself. Being with the animals in the clinic actually felt . . . *natural*.

My skin tingled. I once felt this way at gymnastics practice—that the sport fit my spirit, that each skill and routine felt right.

When did gymnastics start feeling *wrong*? Was it when I grew taller than the other girls? Or advanced to Level 5? Or was it something else—something inside of me that had changed?

Hamlet's hooves clicked against the smooth tiles as she trotted down the hall to check on us. I sat down and wrapped my arms around her neck. "Dr. Stern," I said, looking up. She was wiping down medical equipment in an examination room. Lucy took a seat beside me on the floor. "Can I ask you a question?"

She met my eyes. "Sure."

"Do you think my family should keep Hamlet?"

She paused, but it didn't seem like she was thinking through her answer. It sorta felt like she was studying me, the way Dad sizes up Tom's teammates, trying to figure out what skills each player was going to bring to the team. "That's not up to me to decide, Josie."

I sighed. "Yeah. I guess not."

Dr. Stern studied her university diploma, which was framed and hanging on the opposite wall. Then her gaze followed the cages down the hall, where we heard Oliver pawing at his little door and the meow of Atticus.

"You know," the vet said thoughtfully, "whenever I need to think something through, I ask the animals their advice."

I raised my eyebrows. "You *do?*"

She nodded, her face serious. "Sometimes people do more talking than listening. It can be difficult to hear my own thoughts through the noise."

I nodded. I understood exactly what she meant. "But it's not like animals can talk back," I said. "They can't actually *give* advice."

"I wish they could!" chimed in Lucy. "Then I'd just

172

have to convince my mom to get a cat. I don't have any brothers or sisters or animals to talk to. . . . It's so unbelievably lonely at my house."

I bit the inside of my cheek. Lonely? I'd always thought Lucy's life was perfect. She went to a fancy private school and had a beautiful townhouse and gymnastics came so easy for her. Both her parents were super involved in everything she did—it was obvious she was the most important person in the world to them. I'd always been envious of her life. Lucy never seemed lost or invisible.

But . . . *lonely?*

I hardly ever felt that, and even when I did, I never was, not *really*. Amelia was always around, ready to jump on furniture or sprint down the sidewalk. Sarah might have an attitude problem, but she loved to joke around and make people laugh. Ellen's face was always stuck in a book, but her eyes lit up if I told her a story. And my brother Tom? Even though he was off at college, I could always call him when I wanted to talk.

And even during the times I needed space from my siblings, Sugar would wag her tail and come sit at my feet. I thought of Hamlet, too. She'd made herself right at home within all our Shilling family chaos. She oinked when I came home from school and raised her snout in greeting. When I gave her baths, she blew bubbles in my face, making me laugh.

As stressful as my family felt sometimes, I couldn't imagine not having my brother and sisters and animals around. I offered Lucy a smile.

"You don't need to feel lonely," I told my best friend. "You have me and you can come over anytime you want!"

"I know, Josie," she said, beaming. "And thanks."

Dr. Stern smiled, too. "You're right, Josie, that animals can't voice their thoughts the way humans can," she continued. "But if you're really quiet, and you pay close attention, I think you'll be surprised by what you can hear."

Goose bumps sprung to life on my arms. This whole time I'd been talking to everyone around me about the pig. But never *once* had I asked Hamlet what she wanted.

For almost a month now, I'd fed Hamlet meals, walked her outside, given her baths, and cleaned her Cave. She trusted me. I desperately wanted to save her life. But selfishly I also wanted to keep Hamlet.

Was I really helping her by trying to keep her?

Maybe Dr. Stern was onto something here. Maybe Hamlet knew where to find her forever home and I'd been too busy making noise.

I stared into Hamlet's deep, dark eyes. I just needed to find some peace and quiet so I could ask her the right questions and listen to what she had to say.

Chapter 16

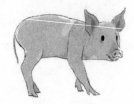

COLD HANDS, WARM HEART

On the eve of my big gymnastics meet, my chattering teeth jolted me awake in the middle of the night. I rubbed my eyes. My fingertips felt like icicles against my skin. The city streets outside seemed eerily quiet, hardly a car whooshing by. Moonlight peeked in through our white window curtain, casting a gray, ghostly glow across our bedroom.

What time was it?

Across the room, Sarah and Ellen were sound asleep in their bunk bed. I leaned over the railing and peeked below. A pillow hid Amelia's face, but the sounds of her soft snores reached my ears.

Something seemed off in the night, like when I'm standing at one end of the balance beam and about to do a straddle jump, but my nerves shake my balance and tip me over the edge.

Hamlet.

I needed to make sure she was okay.

My heart raced in my chest as I swung my legs over the bed, toes curling around each rung of the ladder as I stepped down to the carpet. I breezed down the hall and past my parents' open bedroom door, where I could see them sleeping in their bed with Sugar snuggled up on the shag carpet rug.

A floorboard squeaked beneath my feet. Sugar's eyes fluttered open, and she cocked her head sideways. I held my breath, praying she wouldn't bark. She just watched me, unblinking.

Oh! She wanted to come with me.

I looked back down the dark hallway toward the staircase and then glanced back at Sugar. Fear was crawling out of my skin. Can dogs smell fear? All of a sudden I didn't care if she barked and woke my family. I needed her to come with me, or I might get too scared and run back to bed. I gave our golden retriever a little wave of permission. She popped up on her feet and followed me down the hall to the stairway.

My heartbeat echoed deep in my ears. Ellen's

hand-me-down sleep shirt—once long enough to reach my ankles—now grazed the skin of my knees. My hand reached for the light switch like it had a mind of its own. No! I pulled it back, as if the wall was fire. I didn't want to wake the family. Not at this hour, on this night, just before Sarah's PSAT in the morning and my big gymnastics meet in the afternoon.

A shiver made the hair beneath my messy low ponytail stand on end. I needed to go downstairs. Cold air tingled in my lungs. Everything was fine. I was just being a baby. Amelia probably left a window open downstairs. I should just go and shut it and peek in on Hamlet. No big deal.

Sugar brushed against me, and the shock of her soft fur made me practically jump out of my skin. "Sugar!" I whispered, ruffling her ears. My eyes adjusted to the darkness until finally I could make out the shape of the banister. I reached for it and moved down the steps, slowly at first, and then faster until I reached the almost pitch-black hallway downstairs.

I twisted the knob on the small table lamp by the front door. The house looked normal with Amelia's scarf and boots by the door, a bazillion coats and hats hanging on the coat rack, and stacks of paper advertisements piled up in the corner, just waiting for Ellen to stuff the Sunday papers for her route. Even from my angle, I could see the bolts locked on the front door.

Everything was fine.

Wasn't it?

I rushed down the hall to Hamlet's Cave, Sugar's nails clicking against the pinewood floors behind me. The baby gate had been knocked down. Newspapers were strewn about. Her water bowl had flipped upside down, melting the ink across the front page of yesterday's *City Centennial*. Square tiles had been ripped off the floor, exposing the old hardwood floor. Her Cave had been completely trashed!

But then I realized it.

Hamlet was gone!

It felt like my heart might explode from pounding so fast. I spun around toward the kitchen. The fridge door was closed, and the floor and counters seemed spotless. Dad must've cleaned it the night before. It didn't look like Hamlet had gotten into anything.

Oh no!

What if she had escaped?

I rushed to the back door and spun the knob. Locked. There's no way Hamlet could've gotten out. A window *had* to be open—that was the only explanation.

No no no no.

Doug's colorful, twinkling lights caught my attention. The living room!

I sprinted out of the kitchen and through the dining room. Our Douglas fir was beautiful in all its glorious lights and popcorn trim, but it looked different somehow, like a bit of Tree Day's magic had fizzled away. It took me another second to figure it out.

Our presents were gone.

We'd been robbed!

And someone had stolen Hamlet!

"Hello?" said a deep voice behind me.

I screamed and spun around, doing a high kick in the air. Tom sat up on the couch, his hair sticking out in all directions.

"Whoa, whoa—Josie?"

"*Tom!*" I gasped. "You scared me half to death!"

"Geez, how'd you learn to kick so high? You could've taken off my head!"

"Sorry! But what're you doing here?!"

"Caught the last bus home and crashed on the couch. . . . What's going on?"

This couldn't be happening. This had to be some

terrible dream. "We were robbed, Tom! And Hamlet's missing!"

My brother rubbed his eyes. "Huh?"

"The presents. They're all gone. Well, except for one, that little one in the corner. Amelia counted them all yesterday. Nineteen. Now look—almost zero!"

Tom squinted his eyes like he was trying to see through his sleepiness. "Dad probably just moved them so Amelia would stop being so nosy."

"No." I shook my head. "That's not it. I know it. And—and they took Hamlet, too!"

"Josie? Tom?"

"Is everything okay?"

Mom and Dad stood at the bottom of the stairs. Mom wrapped a bathrobe more tightly around her chest, and Dad's eyebrows furrowed together in concern.

My lower lip began to shake. "Hamlet's gone—"

"Hamlet's right there, sweetie." Mom motioned to the corner of the room. The pig was snuggled up inside a big wicker basket where all the folded blankets are stored. She had burrowed her body inside the fabrics, so only her snout was exposed.

Dad sighed. "Oh, honey. We haven't been robbed. Just go back to sleep, okay? It's the middle of the night."

I rushed to Hamlet's side and lifted the blankets, just to see for myself that she wasn't hurt. She opened her eyes and nestled her cold snout against me. "She's freezing!" I exclaimed, taken aback. "She must've busted out of her Cave to get warm." I pulled the blankets back up over her body, exhaling a sigh of relief that even though she was cold, she seemed fine.

"It *is* freezing in here, Stephen. I'll check the thermostat." Mom rubbed her arms vigorously and moved down the hall. "Fifty-eight degrees. Oh, my goodness. Fifty-eight degrees! Stephen! What happened?"

"Hmmm. Could be a number of things." Dad leaned forward, examining the thermostat more closely. "I'll have a technician come out to take a look at it. Tom, please grab the space heater and get it running down here. It's in the coat closet on the bottom shelf."

"I'll check on the girls," Mom said.

Tom nodded, and Sugar trotted off alongside him while Mom disappeared upstairs. "But Dad." I got to my feet and motioned toward the tree again. "The *presents*—"

"They weren't stolen, Josie." Dad wrapped his arm around my shoulders and gave me a squeeze, the way he always does when he's about to deliver bad news, like that time he told me I couldn't go to private school with Lucy. "The presents were returned."

He said it like they hijacked the van and drove themselves back to the store. I blinked. "You *returned* them? But why?"

Dad pinched his lips together. "This might be hard for you to understand right now, but we had to take them all back. We—we—" He cleared his throat. "We maxed out a credit card and . . . I'm so sorry, honey, but we can't afford presents this Christmas."

I stared at him, too stunned to say anything. It's not like I expected much—but still. I thought there'd be *something*. I tried not to cry when I met Dad's eyes.

"Okay," was all I could manage.

Dad exhaled. "I'll go make some calls and figure out what's going on with our heating system."

"Okay," I said again.

And with that, I was alone in the living room with Hamlet, with a terrible feeling in the pit of my stomach as if I drank too much eggnog. I grabbed a patchwork pillow off the couch and punched it, plopping down on the floor next to Hamlet, unfolding her blanket so it stretched across us both.

I needed to get my rest. Tomorrow was the big day.

Maybe the biggest day of my *life*. But I couldn't stop staring at the tree lights, a million thoughts and emotions whirling through my mind. Everything just felt so *heavy* inside.

Hamlet climbed out of the basket and snuggled up next to me like she knew I needed a friend right now. Her body was *massive*. I couldn't believe she'd once been this little piglet that I cradled in my arms. I had to grab another blanket to cover my bare legs.

"Oh, Hammie." I sighed and rested my head on the pillow. I scratched behind Hamlet's ears until her eyes slowly closed.

Although the curtains were drawn over the living room window, from my angle on the floor I saw a slice of night sky outside. Soft, white snow fell against the glass. I caught the glimmer of a streetlamp and passing headlights. It was hard to imagine this big world out there, with other families and people with their own problems and worries.

Hamlet stared at me. I quit petting her head and she nuzzled her snout against my cheek, making me laugh. "Oh, Hamlet," I said again into her twitching ear. "It's like the holidays are falling apart. . . . And my gymnastics meet is tomorrow of *all* days, and I should be

resting, but I can't stop thinking about all this *stuff*. . . ."
I exhaled a big breath. "And I don't know what to do
about—about you. You're the best pig in the world,
even when you don't listen to me. . . ."

The Christmas tree lights flickered in Hamlet's dark
eyes, and it was a strange blend of happiness and sadness.
I felt like I was disappointing her. I thought about what
Dr. Stern told me yesterday, about her talking to animals
to ask their advice. Hamlet blinked, as if waiting.

"Hamlet . . ." I whispered slowly. "Where do *you*
want to live?"

I don't know what I expected to happen. It's not
like pigs can talk, and I didn't hear any voices in my
head, like you read about in books. But what *did* happen totally surprised me and gave me the exact answer
I was looking for.

Hamlet stood on all fours, trotted to the big window, and reared up on her back legs. Her front hooves
clunked against the windowpane. She looked at me,
blinking.

I waited, listening.

Hamlet turned to the window and squealed a big,
throaty, high-pitched sound like I'd never heard before
in my entire life.

SOO WEEEEEEEEE!

It sounded like a pig crying.

It was then that I realized it. Hamlet might love me, but she didn't want to live here in the city. She wanted to be outside, where she'd be free to be curious and roam around, not confined inside a tiny city townhouse with seven humans she'd only just met.

Hamlet wanted freedom.

My eyes welled up with tears. I waved her back to the floor. "Okay, Hammie," I said as she hoofed it across the living room. "Maybe I was holding on to this idea of keeping you and not really working to find you a new family. I'm—I'm sorry, Hamlet. Forgive me, okay? I'll find you the most perfect home ever. . . . We still have sixteen days. Don't you worry about a thing."

She snuggled up next to me on the floor. I stared up into Doug's colorful branches, tugged a candy cane off the tree, and peeled off the plastic wrapper. I handed the candy cane to Hamlet, and she eagerly crunched it in between her teeth and then licked my face with her minty-fresh breath.

I laughed. "Oh, Hamlet," I said, my chest swelling with warmth and sadness all at the same time.

"Everything will be okay. I promise."

I tried my hardest to believe that. I wrapped my arms around the pig's thick neck and fell asleep with the thump of her calm heartbeat vibrating in my ears.

Chapter 17

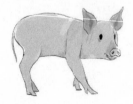

STOP, LOOK, AND LISTEN

Sometimes winter break can be boring, but when you have to hold splits for three minutes on each side several times a day, visualize your gymnastics routines, scrub slushy snow off the bottom of your workout bag, and take care of a farm pig growing *much* too quickly, it's like there are never enough minutes in the day.

Today was the big day: my gymnastics meet. While the family was having breakfast and Sarah was off taking the PSAT, I looped the bike chain around Sully's front gate and spread the word that it was time for an emergency meeting at the Three Stoops.

"We don't have much time before warm-ups," Lucy reminded me, kicking snow off her boots. "Mom said we need to leave at eleven to get to the gym in time."

"Yep." I tugged my wool hat over my ears to keep them warm. "You guys, we need to brainstorm—and fast," I told the gang after everyone arrived. I drew in a deep breath, filling my lungs up, and exhaled. "We're abandoning the Case for Keeping Hamlet."

"Wait—what?" Fernanda raised an eyebrow. "We can't give up yet!"

I nodded, more confident than ever that this was the right thing to do. "We have to. It's time for Operation Home for Hamlet."

Sully spun his notebook to the Case File while I updated the gang on Hamlet's escape and what happened with Mrs. Taglioni's fence and the pie incident with Dad's boss.

"Whoa," Carlos said. "Hamlet can jump that high? With those short legs?"

"*And* she's fast," I told him. "Lightning fast!"

"I still can't believe Hammie flipped that pie on that mean lady's sweater!" Lucy said.

I shook my head. "Yeah, me neither." I filled them in on how Hamlet knocked the baby gate over the other day, pulled up the floor tiles in her Cave, and how I could barely lift her out of the bathtub these days, even though I'd been doing all my gymnastics conditioning.

"And there's something else . . ." I brushed the thin layer of snow off the top step and sat down. "I asked Hamlet what she wanted. Like *really* asked her, and looked in her eyes, and listened and everything, just as Dr. Stern suggested. Hammie jumped on the windowsill and starting squealing toward the glass, and then I realized it . . . she doesn't want to be a city pig, even if I wish I could keep her. We have to close the Case File, and I need your help to find her a forever home—and fast."

Everyone was silent for a moment, absorbing the news. Finally, Fernanda nodded in agreement, and the rest of our friends did the same. "Hmmm," said Sully. Then he drew a big *X* across the Case File, flipping to a new page. He handed his notebook to Carlos. At the top of the new page, Carlos carefully wrote *Operation Home for Hamlet* in big, swirly, cursive, making the start of a new investigation official.

"You came to the right place," Fernanda said cheerfully. "We'll help you."

"Yeah," Carlos said. "What if we divided up the phone book and called every animal sanctuary in the county?"

"That's a good idea." I nodded. "On Monday I'll ask

Ms. Fischer if we can photocopy the pages."

Even though we didn't all go to the same school, we all knew Ms. Fischer. She was the local librarian and the nicest lady on the planet. She always smelled like oatmeal cookies and wore her hair short, just above the ears.

"Carlos said *county*. What about in the state?" Sully chewed on his pencil, deep in thought.

"That's so gross," Carlos said, making a face. Fernanda laughed and Sully looked up from the page, his cheeks turning red.

"What if I help make posters?" Carlos suggested. "We're doing color theory now in my art class. I can ask my teacher which color is the most eye-catching. So people walking down the street will *really* notice the poster, you know?"

"Oh! That's a good idea. I can email you one of my photos of Hamlet to put on it, too," Lucy added, pulling out her phone.

Fernanda snapped her fingers, her face lighting up. "I'm learning Photoshop in my Girls in Technology club." She looked at her brother. "Maybe after dinner tonight we can put everything together in a document? This will be fun. The pig emojis are my favorite ones!"

"We can print them at my place if you want," added Sully. "I'll help hang them around the neighborhood."

"That sounds good. Thanks, guys!" I checked my watch. "Lucy and I gotta go."

"Good luck today!" said Fernanda.

"See you there!" said Sully.

I spun around in surprise. "Wait, you're coming to the meet today?"

"Um, yeah." Sully glanced at our friends, his cheeks turning red again. "We're all going! The twins' dad is driving us."

"Yay!" said Lucy, and I grinned.

As a visiting team at Oasis Gymnastics Center, my team got to warm up first. I bounced in place and stretched my limbs, waking up every muscle and joint in my body. "Arm circles!" Coach instructed, and my teammates obeyed, going through every step of our usual warm-up. "Push-ups! Belly in, eyes up if you can. Stomach in! Two . . . three . . ."

It felt good to move my body, even though I felt awkward and gangly. It helped free me from my electrified nerves and worries circulating in my brain.

"One-minute handstands," Coach said. "Starting

NOW! Squeeze those thighs, girls! Knees together, point those toes! Think TALL!"

I stretched my fingers, palms pressing into the gray fabric of the floor. I would've laughed if I weren't holding my breath in my cheeks. I was *always* thinking tall. I didn't need Coach to remind me. Especially not now, when our meet was about to begin.

Josie Long Legs.

Upside down, my long ponytail grazed the floor and my face turned hot from blood pooling into my head. Coach counted out loud until finally she said, "Okay, girls, get some water and let's meet back at the beam in two."

I touched my toes to the floor and stood up, following my team.

"You ready?" Lucy asked me, swigging from her water bottle as we stood by the visitors' lockers.

I nodded. "As ready as I'll ever be."

"Same here." Lucy grinned. "Glad beam is first! We'll get it out of the way."

Lucy and I were both pretty good at beam, but a few skills tripped us up. I did well on the tumbling passes, like the back walkovers, because they were fast and I had the control. It was the spins and turns that made me nervous, where I had to be graceful and focused and needed to slow down my body and mind. Slowing things down gave me time to doubt. I shook out my hands and crackled my knuckles.

Mind over matter.

We jogged over to the beam with our Level 5 team. We looked like a flock of glittering birds in our matching sparkling blue leotards, the special competition ones with the long sleeves that we never get to wear to practice.

I glanced into the bleachers. Ellen was already sitting up there with Mom, and it didn't look like she brought a book with her. Her eyes scanned the facility, and when our eyes made contact she waved at me. I waved back. Tom arrived, weaving through the crowd to climb up and sit next to her. When he spotted me, he gave me a thumbs-up.

No sign of Dad and my other sisters yet. Sarah must still be at the PSAT. Heat bloomed inside my chest. I inhaled deeply, the thick scent of sweat mixed with chalk filling my nostrils.

"Circle round, girls," Coach said. She brought her palms together in front of her chest. "Almost time to march in. How're we feeling today?"

Maxie and I made eye contact. We both burst out laughing. "Nervous!" Maxie said, and I grinned.

"Me, too," I said, shaking out my wrists.

"Me three!" chimed in Lucy.

"Terrified!" admitted Shelby.

"Same," said Becky, rising on her toes.

The other girls giggled. With each laugh, I felt my body relaxing a bit. Coach smiled. "That's all normal. As you know, there are some competitive gyms here today. Excellence, Oasis, and Grandview all have top-notch teams. I was watching the Oasis girls warm up on floor—they're strong. All of them landed their front tucks." Next to me, Taryn exhaled loudly. "But we've trained hard for this, and you girls are ready. Becky, remember to stretch up and pull those knees to your chest! Don't waste time getting into your tucks, it'll delay your rotation. Lucy, think fast fast FAST on the bars! You'll wow the judges with your connections." Coach turned to me. "Don't hunch your shoulders— there you go. Stand tall. Chin up. And Josie . . ." She gave my ponytail a playful tug. "Stop fretting so much."

My cheeks burned. "It's that obvious?"

Coach laughed. "Just free your mind and you'll maintain your balance," she said, pinpointing my greatest fear today: losing my focus and wavering on skills that I *know* I'm capable of doing well. I nodded. Coach didn't know everything going on at home, but she knew me well enough to recognize that I was a worrier. She clapped her hands, drawing the team together. Music floated through the high rafters of the gym, signaling that it was almost time for the march in, when all the teams were introduced.

"We're here to show them what we've got," Coach said, "but let's not forget to have fun, too—okay, girls?"

We nodded and brought our hands together for our Team Universal cheer. The excitement in the gym was thick. You could feel it tingling across your arms, like a thunderstorm was igniting around us, but we hadn't felt that first cool drop of water yet.

I smiled at Lucy, placing my palm on top of her knuckles. We all crowded close and yelled, "GO, UNIVERSAL, GO!" before raising our hands high into the air.

"Okay, Josie, you're on beam first," Coach said, nodding my way. I checked my posture, pretending an invisible string was pulling my heart toward the sky.

I'd done these routines loads of times before. Maybe *thousands* of times before. The only difference was that today the bleachers were crammed with people and there was a panel of judges studying my every move, ready to tally up a score.

All I could do was trust my training. And breathe.

Chapter 18

WE ARE THE CHAMPIONS (OR NOT)

I saluted the judges' table and gracefully approached the beam, pressing my palms onto the smooth, taut leather. My lungs expanded, swelling with oxygen, and I controlled my breath during its exhale, narrowing my vision to the teeny tiny spot between my fingers.

Focus and control. That's all it takes to hit a perfect beam routine.

It's as easy and hard as that simple truth.

I raised myself up onto the beam, swinging a straight leg over and propping myself into a tightly closed *V* sit position. I melted my mind into each movement, remembering to stay light on my feet and keep my eyes on the end of the beam. I didn't waver on my first turn, or when I stepped back, high on my toes, setting up my first jump.

A flash of a camera jolted me back into reality, and suddenly I pulled away from my focus and remembered I was performing in front of a whole group of people. Nerves shot through my body like a million arrows, and my shadow paused on the blue mat below. I began to sweat. *Oh, great.* Now my feet and palms felt slick. What if I slipped off the beam?

I needed more chalk. But I couldn't get off the beam—that'd be a major deduction.

I can't do this I can't do this I can't do this—

I met Coach's eyes. She nodded, urging me on, like the ticking clock beside the judge's table. I'm not sure what was worse, the terrifying silence in the gym, or the fact that I had my first handstand coming up.

This is when I had to be brave and just go for it. I emptied my lungs of air and inhaled again.

Step, step, leap!

I landed solidly on my left leg and held my right behind me as high, active, and steady as I could. *Phew.* That wasn't so bad.

Music began to play in the background as the Oasis

team started their floor routines. I swallowed hard, trying to dissolve the knot in my throat.

Almost done. I've got this.

Arms out, leg back! I leveled down into the first handstand, keeping as strong and tight as I could.

I'm a tree. I'm strong. Nothing can knock me over.

I held the move for a full second—even though my back arched a little at the end—and struck the rest of the skills down one by one. Back walkover. Split jump. Sissonne.

All that was left was a two-second handstand to dismount. I just had to hold it and quarter-turn to dismount onto the mat. I bent down and onto my palms, blood rushing into my head. A camera flashed from the bleachers. The sore skin of my raw palms burned, and a groan escaped my mouth as I pushed hard on the beam, trying to ignore the pain and hold the move for just *another second.* But I twisted my hips too far and lost control, falling onto the mat below and landing on my knees.

Did that even *count* as a dismount?

It was pretty much a total flop.

I leaned back to prop up on my feet. Every routine required a salute, even the not-so-perfect ones. I lifted my chin and saluted the judges, then walked over to my team on the sidelines. The girls muttered, "Good job," and "Way to go, Josie," but I could read through their halfhearted comments.

My beam routine was a disaster.

Coach handed me my water bottle. "Just a little shaky on the dismount, but you kept your cool, Josie. I know there's a lot of pressure today. Just don't let those nerves get the best of you."

I shook out my hands, wrists loose. "A camera flash caught me off guard," I admitted as I watched the scoreboard.

Coach put her arm on my shoulder. "They're there to capture the moment you *shine*. Not the moment you fail. Remember that."

"Right. Mind over matter."

"Exactly."

My score popped up in bright red lights: 8.550 out of ten.

Oh, well. Not the best, but at least it was over. I slipped on my warm-up pants to watch the rest of the girls compete. "C'mon, Becky!" I cheered as my teammate approached the beam.

Overall, Team Universal did decent on the beam

rotation and even better on floor. It felt like back tucks were coming easily these days, for all my teammates and me, now that we'd gained confidence in the skill.

Run, hurdle, roundoff, back handspring, and *pounce*!

I soared through the air, tucking my knees to my chest, and landing solidly with my hands graceful above my head.

I went into vault feeling good. I'd almost forgotten about everyone in the stands and the judges tallying up deductions. And even though my vault warm-up passes were stronger than my actual one for score, I didn't get *that* many deductions, and I actually had fun.

But as the teams rotated for the final time and we lined up alongside the uneven bars, that terrible knot in my throat reappeared. Bars meant two whole minutes of feeling my calluses pinch and break beneath Lucy's old grips.

I studied my best friend as she took her turn on bars. Lucy was just *soaring* today during warm-ups. The way she could whip and swing and release from bar to bar made my jaw drop. She made it look so easy!

I gave her a big hug and helped tighten the dark, springy coils in her loosened ponytail. "That was awesome!" I told her, and she grinned, her face luminous.

While I waited my turn to warm up, I looked up into the stands. My whole family was here now except for Sarah. I swore I saw her up there earlier during the last rotation. Maybe I was wrong. Mom's face looked relaxed as she scanned the sea of gymnasts, clutching her camera with both hands. Dad had a focused expression while he watched my team warm up.

The Three Stoops crew sat next to the twins' dad. Sully adjusted his baseball cap. When our eyes met, he gave me a huge, goofy grin. Heat flared at my cheeks.

I'd known Sully for, like, *years*. But something in his tone seemed different when he made that comment about my back tuck being awesome. It wasn't a big deal. Right? And it was cool that he came out to support Lucy and me at our meet.

Then why did I suddenly feel more nervous?

Was it even *possible* to feel more nervous right now?

I stepped up to the bars and gave a few relaxed swings before kipping up to the low bar. My warm-up routine went fine—maybe a little loosey goosey, but I couldn't break free of my fears. All those eyes on me. All those people probably noticing how tall I was compared to the other girls, how wrong I looked for this sport.

Josie Long Legs.

I wanted to throw up.

"Gather round, girls," Coach said, snapping my attention back to the team. "We're in solid standing going into our final apparatus." She spoke slowly, emphasizing each word. "It's time to focus on our energy on this last routine. Ready?"

"Ready!" we echoed.

Not ready, I thought. My palms felt slimy, and I chalked them up some more before slipping on my tattered grips. I was never going to feel ready.

Taryn went first. Strong as usual. I bounced on the sidelines, rolling up on my toes and back on my heels. My turn was last. It was like my worst nightmare coming true: all this extra time to worry. The gym suddenly felt too hot, and I needed air. I fanned myself with my palm, trying to ignore everything haunting me inside.

Chalk could get in my eyes.

The judges could score me a zero.

I could slip and break my arm.

Team Universal could lose this whole competition because of *me*.

"Pssssst! Josie!" a voice whispered. I spun around. A head popped up from behind a stack of mats off to the side.

"Sarah?" I wrinkled my nose. "What're you doing here?"

My older sister looked both ways like she was crossing a busy street and rushed to my side. She slapped something in my hand, making me yelp from the sting of it. "Watch it!" I hissed. "I can't get hurt before my routine!"

"I'm not here to hurt you, sis. I'm here to *help* you."

"What?"

"Just open it already!"

I realized I was holding a package loosely wrapped in ruled notebook paper. It looked like it'd been crumpled up in the bottom of her book bag. I tore at an end until I touched something firm. I blinked.

"Grips?" I said, bringing them closer to my eyes. I couldn't believe it. "These are grips! Where in the world did these come from?"

Sarah beamed. "Yesterday was payday at work, so Lucy helped me pick out the right size grips. . . . I mean, I'm not sure if you're supposed to break them in like shoes or something, but I figured maybe I shouldn't wait until Christmas to give them to you, like maybe you'd rather have them right now? Hey, what's wrong? Why're you crying?"

I wiped my eyes with the back of my hand. "I'm not crying."

I remembered the package now. It had been the only one remaining under the tree last night, when I'd laid there on the floor with Hamlet. This present was the only one that Dad hadn't returned.

"Did I buy the wrong ones?"

"No! Not at all. They're perfect." I wrapped my arms around Sarah's neck and gave her a big squeeze. "Thank you. Thank you so much! You have no idea what this means to me. . . ."

My voice cracked. It wasn't just the grips. It was that Sarah *noticed* me in the chaos of the house with everything else going on, the house heat going out, the drama with Mrs. Taglioni, all the mischief with Hamlet, Tom's football stardom, Ellen's straight As on her finals, and Amelia's bubbly energy that captured everyone's attention.

Sarah still saw *me*.

"Your palms have been gross for weeks. It was about time someone clunked over some coin for new grips, and we all know where *your* allowance savings went." Sarah's tone was light. "Now. Get those things on, and go make your big sister proud." I nodded, and Sarah disappeared into a sea of gymnasts, weaving back toward the bleachers.

I unbuckled Lucy's old grips from my wrists and tossed them in the garbage.

Sarah bought me new grips.

I had new grips!

My heart could've burst right then and there. Suddenly I couldn't wait to swing from the bars. I was so excited, I barely felt the cracked blisters sting on my palms anymore. I was going to show everyone—Coach, the team, my family, friends, and *myself*—how hard I'd worked on bars, and that I deserved to be here.

I worked too hard for this.

"Next up, Josie Shilling for Team Universal, on the uneven bars!" announced a voice.

I clapped my hands together. A cloud of chalk dust floated up into the air as I walked over and saluted the judges.

I was ready.

With laser-beam focus, I pounced from a springboard to the lower bar, keeping my legs tight and piked. I glide kipped to the bar until I was balanced upright on straight arms. The grips were more rigid than Lucy's worn-in ones, but the tightness around my wrists felt good, and the unforgiving leather made me feel in control.

I swung around the lower bar again until finally I tucked my knees to my chest to squat on the bar, arms out, reaching. My heart skipped a beat as I jumped into the air and caught the high bar.

Everything around me—the gym, faces, lights—blurred as I focused in on the bar, swinging, swinging, swinging, my ponytail flipping ahead of my body. The bar gave a slight bend as I changed directions, and a rush of cool air whipped at my cheeks.

"C'mon Josie!" my teammates yelled.

The final skill was a flyaway dismount.

I dropped down into a dead hang and swung back and forth. When my toes soared forward, I kept my body long and tight and released the bar. I could hear Coach's voice in my head—*look for the mat!*—and I tossed my head back, eyes on the ground, as I finished the skill.

Plastic crackled beneath my feet as I landed hard, knees bent, arms straight out. I stuck it! I felt my face light up as I raised my arms high and saluted the judges.

My team jumped up and down, rushing to my side, screaming. Lucy hugged me tight. "That was AMAZING!"

"Let's see what the judges thought," I said breathlessly, but I couldn't wipe the grin off my face.

"Wow, Josie!" Coach exclaimed, clapping me on the back. "That's the best bars routine I've ever seen you do! I'm so proud of you."

"Thanks," I said. "I felt strong today."

"You looked strong," Coach said. "But even better, you looked confident."

I nodded. It wasn't the new grips from Sarah or that a million people were watching my every move. It was that I believed in myself. Confidence felt *awesome*.

My score appeared: 9.85.

I felt my shoulders sag a little. Not a perfect ten. But as I unbuckled my grips from my hands, I realized that I still felt great. I'd done my absolute best, and it was one of my top scores on bars, even though I just learned these skills and they were much harder than my old Level 4 bars routine.

I lifted my chin and looked to the stands. Sully pumped his fist and the twins screamed, and my whole family was standing and cheering. Dad clapped slow and dramatic, like each time his palms came together he was trying a little harder to hold back supportive tears. Tom pointed at me and yelled, "Yeahhhh, JoJo!"

and all my sisters clutched each other and jumped up and down while my mom snapped pictures and waved.

I just stared, taking it all in.

"Wow," Lucy whispered next to me. "You're so lucky to have a big family rooting for you. I mean, look at all of them! They're so proud of you!"

I grinned. Lucy was right. Us Shillings might drive each other wild and be too loud for our own good, but I loved each and every one of them, no matter what.

"Yeah," I said, waving back to my family as Mom snapped another picture. Then I hugged my best friend. She was family, too, after all. "Definitely lucky."

Chapter 19

LAW & ORDER

The doorbell was ringing, over and over again. I fluttered my eyes open. Where *was* everyone? It was holiday break, so usually someone was around.

Ding dong!

Ugh. I guess I'd get it. I swung my feet onto the bunk bed ladder and climbed down. By the time I rushed to the door, I was out of breath and still half-asleep. "Yes?" I said, swinging the door open wide.

Two police officers stood on our front stoop.

"Um, hello," I said, the surprise visitors catching me off guard. "How can I help you?"

"Good morning. Are your parents home?" asked the policewoman.

"I don't—"

"I'm right here, Josie. Sorry to keep you waiting, officers. I was wrapping up a phone call and we weren't expecting anyone," Mom said. "Is there something I can help you with?"

"You're Mrs. Shilling?" the policeman asked, flipping his wallet open and revealing an official badge.

"Yes."

"I'm Officer Brady," he said, "and this is Officer Chou." He pointed at the policewoman. "We're investigating a report that livestock is living within your home?"

I stole a glance behind me, where Hamlet rested in her Cave. She was within view of the front door, if I opened it wide enough. Oh no—either Ms. Coburn or Mrs. Taglioni had complained about Hamlet. This was bad news. *Very* bad news.

Please don't take my pig away please don't take my pig away please don't take my pig away please please please please . . .

Mom's jaw clenched. "Yes, that's correct. We have a pig named Hamlet."

"Hamlet?" said Officer Chou.

Mom pulled the door wide open on its hinges and motioned down the hall, where newspapers stuck out from beneath the stairs. My skin tingled. I'd seen Hamlet's snout just a moment earlier. Where was she now?

"Can I inquire as to why exactly you're here, Officer Brady, Officer Chou?"

"Are you aware that under City Law 26 Section B it's illegal to keep livestock within the city limits?" asked Officer Brady.

It felt like the blood drained from my face. *Illegal?* To keep Hamlet?

Oh no!

"No, I wasn't," Mom replied, her eyes widening. "But we aren't keeping her. We're only temporarily caring for her until our daughter Josie can find her a permanent home."

"That's me," I explained, placing a palm over my heart. "I'm Josie."

"I see." Officer Chou's eyes wandered down the hallway. "Mind if we come inside for a minute?"

"Not at all. Be my guest." Mom waved her hand again. We moved to the side as the police officers entered our home and approached Hamlet's Cave.

"MOM! I can't find my other boot!" cried Amelia, sliding down the banister and clobbering me at the bottom of the steps.

"Millie!" I snapped.

A goofy grin plastered her face as we got to our feet. "Sor-*ry*."

"Amelia!" Mom scolded. "We have visitors. And where one boot is, the other one can't be far."

"Visitors?" Amelia looked around blankly until her eyes rested on the police officers in the hall. "Oh! Sor-RY!"

"It's okay. We've only just arrived," said Officer Brady with a smile. "Besides, I lose a boot all the time. So where did you say the pig is?"

"In there," I said, feeling the hair on the back of my neck spring to life. As I approached Hamlet's Cave, I could see that she was nowhere in sight, but her baby gate was still intact. Uh oh. Did she jump *this* fence too?!

"Josie, did you let Hamlet upstairs in the girls' room again?" asked Mom, raising an eyebrow. She leaned over the baby gate, inspecting the floor, where the newspapers had shifted. "Did Hamlet *pull up the floor tiles?*"

A warm sensation crept up my throat.

"Found it!" Amelia's voice echoed throughout the downstairs. "It was in the kitchen and *not* near the other one *for the record*!"

"Pigs don't just disappear," reasoned Officer Brady. "I'm sure it's around here somewhere."

The most terrific crash reached our ears. Amelia screamed. The police officers raced into the kitchen, Mom and I following at their heels.

I couldn't help but burst out laughing at what I saw.

Amelia stood on the kitchen counter, clutching a fly swatter in her hand. The fridge door was swung wide open. Hamlet furiously rooted through the packaged foods and bottled drinks, yanking them out by her teeth. Milk spilt across the kitchen tiles and the smell of cracked raw eggs filled the air.

Mom's mouth fell slack, unable to find the words to explain what had just happened. I choked back my laugh as the horror set in. What if they took her away right now? Oh no oh no oh no.

Officer Chou wrapped her arms around Hamlet's neck, tugging her back from the fridge.

"Looks like your livestock has a big appetite," said Officer Brady, hooking his thumbs on his belt loop. Hamlet met my eyes, and she squirmed her big, round, pink body, as if asking for a hug.

There was absolutely *no* chance I was going to hug that bad pig right now!

My body felt numb, but I found the strength to nod. "Yeah, she's . . . uh . . . a big eater."

"And she *pushed* me *over*!" wailed Amelia, shaking the fly swatter like it was a sword.

"Oh, sweetie. Are you okay?" asked Mom, looking up. I'd practically forgotten Amelia was up there! Mom wrapped her arms around Amelia, lifting her back down to the floor. Amelia nodded, but she glared at me like it was my fault.

Right then Hamlet's teeth sunk into a can of soda, making it fizz all over Officer Chou's pants. I swear Mom's face turned white as a ghost as she reached for paper towels and dabbed at the fabric.

"Just a little Diet Coke," Mom said lightly.

"Why don't we put the pig back in its pen and talk a little more," suggested Officer Brady. Once Hamlet was secured in her Cave, the officers toured our home. They didn't say much besides asking questions like, "Is this your only dog? I see your backyard is fenced, is the gate to the alley locked? Is that a new piece of wood along the far side?" to which Mom answered each and every one.

"Well, Mrs. Shilling," said Officer Brady as they circled back to the front door. "Everything appears to be shipshape here. It's not like you're an animal hoarder or anything, and I understand you're trying to do right by the pig by finding it a proper home. Looks like your Hamlet is a feisty one, I'll give you that, but she's not a direct menace to society. Since it's Christmas Eve, we're not going to call animal control, but understand this is a serious warning that the pig *must* be out by the year's end, or we'll have the animal removed from your home and penalize you with a fine. I'm sorry, but pigs just aren't allowed in the city. You have eight days."

Officer Chou handed my mom a business card with her contact information.

"Eight days. Understood," said Mom, turning the card over in her hand. "Thank you for waiting until the holiday season is over. Good-bye."

After the officers left, Mom turned to face me. She didn't even need to give me a lecture. The thought of the city animal control snatching up Hamlet and carting her away to a bacon farm filled me with absolute terror.

"Don't worry, Mom," I promised her, touching her wrist. "I'm working on it."

Chapter 20

HOME FOR THE HOLIDAYS

That night my parents called a family meeting. My siblings and I fought for a seat on the couch cushions while Mom snuggled up with Sugar on the carpet, gently stroking back her soft, floppy ears.

"Wait!" I bolted upright from between Sarah and Ellen, losing my spot on the cushiest cushion. "Everyone's here but Hamlet. She deserves to be here, too."

Dad shook his head. "No pigs in the living room."

"Broke that rule a long time ago," deadpanned Sarah.

"Breaking a rule doesn't make the rule nonexistent," argued Ellen. "It makes the rule *irrelevant*."

"Ughhhh, we know, we know, you got straight As on your report card, genius," said Sarah, rolling her eyes.

Mom calmly raised up hand. "Girls, please stop arguing."

"She started it," said Ellen.

"This is family time," Mom said, and Ellen's open mouth snapped shut.

Amelia's eyes lit up. "So Hamlet's officially part of the family?"

"No. Hamlet's an intruder," said Sarah. "Legally speaking."

Tom raised his palm in the air, mimicking Mom a moment earlier. "Hamlet's a guest—*technically* speaking."

Mom laughed at my brother and patted Sugar's back. "Stephen, I vote Hamlet joins us in the living room."

I met Dad's eyes and realized that he'd been watching me. He gave me one, decisive nod, as if he understood that my time with the pig was short. I rushed to Hamlet's Cave. The gate was now twice as high, because we'd stacked books beneath it. I opened it and let her out.

Hamlet oinked happily as she trotted after me down the hall. She circled on top of the big fleece blanket by the fireplace before lying down, and I bent over and curled up next to her.

Dad began his speech. "As you all know, Christmas is going to be a little different this year . . ."

"You mean cheaper," broke in Sarah.

Ellen shot her a glare. "Way to be compassionate, Sarah."

Tom crossed his arms over his chest, bumping Amelia's cheek with his elbow, making her squawk like a rubber chicken. "Oh—sorry!"

Dad cleared his throat. "*As I was saying* . . . this year is going to be a little different. As you guys know, we had to return the presents this year. But your mom and I came up with a great idea. We're going to do a Handmade Christmas."

"Handmade Christmas?" asked Ellen.

"Yes, we're going to make each other presents this year!" added Mom cheerfully.

"Now, there are a few rules . . ." started Dad.

Sarah sighed. "More rules?"

"Yeah, rules aren't fun," Amelia whined.

Dad's cell phone rang again. "Hello, Mother," he said. "Merry Christmas to you, too! Are you still at John's? Yes, yes okay—"

"It's Grandma?" Amelia squealed. "I wanna talk to her!"

"Stop squirming!" Tom said, sliding down from the couch to the floor. I jumped up to claim his spot on the couch, and Hamlet climbed up on my lap. I grunted. She was heavy!

"Can I read for a few more minutes?" Ellen asked Mom. "I'm at a really good part."

"What's it about?" Amelia asked, waiting by Dad's feet to talk to Grandma next.

"Well." Ellen smiled. "A girl on an adventure to find a very *special* gold nugget."

"Why is it special?"

"It's the only thing that can sharpen a magic sword, one that was passed down to her from past generations, and she thinks its power will save her village from the Goblin War."

"Goblin War—*creepy*!"

Sarah chucked popcorn at Amelia, who laughed and tried to catch it in her mouth. After we all had a chance to talk with Grandma, Dad resumed the family meeting. "The rules for Handmade Christmas aren't rules exactly. Consider these *challenges*, okay, kids? Now, first thing . . . no one can spend any money."

I almost brought up the fact that Sarah had already broken that rule with buying me grips, but that seemed different because it hadn't been about Christmas, it had been a gift to help me out. Plus, she'd used her own paycheck.

Dad's cell phone buzzed from atop the mantel and behind the stocking hooks. He glanced at his flashing phone screen.

"Your mother again?" asked Mom. Dad shook his head, and they exchanged a look. Mom's lips pursed together like there was something important left unsaid. His phone buzzed again.

"What if Grandma forgot to tell you something?" I asked him.

"It's not Grandma," Mom and Dad said in unison, and Dad added, "I'll call them back later. Now, what was I saying? Ah, yes, rule number two: the present you give must be made from something that *you* own. Don't take anyone else's belongings, okay? And the last rule: remake that thing into something totally different, something that you think the *other person* would like. Understood?"

I grinned. I'm not super crafty or anything, but this challenge actually sounded like fun.

"Loud and clear," Sarah said.

"Yep!" Amelia said.

Ellen and I nodded, while Tom gave Dad a thumbs-up. Dad held a worn Ohio State Buckeyes hat and extended it toward Mom first. She pulled out a small piece of paper, unfolded it, read it, and then tucked it into her pocket.

"So this is a Handmade *Secret Santa* Christmas?" asked Ellen.

"Exactly." Dad watched as she drew the next name. "It'll be fun to see who can guess who made them a present. So remember, it's a secret!" He cleared his throat again. "And there might be a little surprise in there, too."

"All I Want for Christmas is You" blasted on the radio, and I felt a shiver bolt down my spine, sending a tingle throughout my body. I hugged Hamlet's neck and whispered, "You're such a good piggie" into her ear. She oinked softly and touched her wet snout to my cheek.

"Aw, peanuts! I got my name!" laughed Amelia.

"Just put it back and grab another one," said Mom.

I wondered who got my name in the hat and what they might make me for Handmade Christmas. I'd gotten enough hand-me-downs in my life, but this felt totally different. This felt . . . special. Because you had to think hard about what the other person might like and create something totally new.

I grinned. Handmade Christmas suddenly sounded awesome.

As the hat was passed around, I secretly hoped that Sarah's name would still be in there so I could repay her kindness from yesterday. When it came time for my turn, there was just one scrap of paper left in the hat. I reached for it, carefully opened up the little piece of scrap paper, and read the name.

My jaw dropped.

What in the world?

This had to be a joke. Right? I blinked, reading the name again.

Mrs. Taglioni.

I glanced at Dad, wanting desperately to ask him the question nagging at me, but not wanting to give away my Secret Santa either.

But still.

It was really confusing, and I wasn't sure how I felt about it.

Mrs. Taglioni was going to celebrate Christmas with us?

Chapter 21

HANDMADE CHRISTMAS

Christmas morning was unusually quiet in our house. Even with the aroma of pancakes sizzling in butter floating up the stairs, we were preoccupied combing through our things, trying to figure out what objects we could remake into a gift for somebody else.

Handmade Christmas was harder than I thought it'd be. All I had was random homework papers and projects from school, broken pencils at the bottom of my backpack, an empty allowance mason jar, and some boring toys that were mostly all hand-me-downs anyways.

I stretched out on my bed, staring at the ceiling where old glow-in-the-dark stickers formed the shapes of constellations that probably didn't even exist in real life.

Okay.

I had a few options. I could ignore the challenge and not make a present for Mrs. Taglioni at all, but that seemed really mean. Or I could just create whatever I wanted, even if she didn't like it. But that didn't seem right either. . . .

I kept replaying that day outside on her stoop, when Dr. Stern was leaving and Ralphie her sugar glider had died. I couldn't get the image of Mrs. Taglioni's red, swollen eyes out of my mind.

Poor Mrs. Taglioni.

She hadn't always been the nicest person to my family, but still. Ralphie's death had left her heartbroken. I felt a little bad for her. And I never once thought about what she did on holidays. She never decorated her townhouse with lights or cinnamon brooms or inflatable reindeer. Did she even have family somewhere out there? Did she celebrate Christmas? She was always alone. And no one should have to spend the holidays alone.

But how was I supposed to even know what Mrs. Taglioni would like? I knew maybe five things about her. She hated noise—especially Shilling noise. She liked things super organized, if her pristine backyard was any clue as to the inside of her townhouse.

I bit my lip. What else?

She wore glasses. Carried her handbag with her everywhere. Was always scowling.

I deflated my lungs and it felt like my spirit was deflating, too.

There were the weird animals, too, I guess. Ralphie. Maybe another secret sugar glider inside her house. All those cats. All those plants.

"GOT MINE!" announced Amelia, sliding into our bedroom on her socks. She was still wearing her red-and-black penguin pajamas.

Great. Here I was still brainstorming, and even Amelia had figured out her handmade gift!

"You're not supposed to give anything away," I reminded her.

"I'm not!" She hid her hands behind her back and swayed from side to side. "You almost done?"

"No. Now go away."

"SHEESH!" Amelia stuck her tongue out at me and bolted out the bedroom just as fast as she had zipped in. I swear, that girl should be on Tom's football team— they would score more touchdowns than anyone!

Minutes dragged on as I stared at the ceiling. Ellen

popped in a few minutes later, retrieving a book off her nightstand.

I sighed. *"You're* done too?"

"Oh!" Ellen looked up at the top bunk in surprise. "Hi, Josie. You scared me. I thought everyone was downstairs."

"Ugh. No." I punched my pillow.

"Well . . ." She tucked the book into the back pocket of her jeans. "Good luck. See you later!"

"Yeah, I mean, I KNOW." Sarah breezed through, clutching the cordless house phone tight to her ear. "Wait—*seriously*? He's already asked her to the prom?" She was probably talking to Trisha, Sully's older sister, I guessed. They hadn't always been close friends, but ever since this school year started, it seemed like they were always calling each other and talking about boys. Sarah rummaged through her desk drawers. Open, slam! Open, *slam!*

"Um, hellllo?" I said, throwing my hands in the air. "You're so loud!"

"Oh, Josie." Sarah switched the phone to the other ear, as if the receiver was too hot. "You should make more noise, I didn't even know you were there."

Typical. I rolled onto my side and tried to zone out

Sarah's voice. A wall bookshelf caught my eye. It was my gymnastics shelf—the only little space that I got to decorate with whatever I wanted in this room I shared with my three sisters. My new, shiny trophy now glistened from the center of the shelf, with my favorite old leotards tacked against the wall on either side of it. There were a few dangling ribbons and medals here and there from my old Level 4 meets and a messy stack of DVDs with my favorite clips of Olympics gymnastics routines. Aly Raisman—my favorite gymnast of all time—stretched across a poster in a sky-high jump.

Mrs. Taglioni and I had nothing in common.

She'd probably hate whatever I gave her, no matter what.

But then I spotted it—nearly teetering over on the edge of the shelf, practically hiding behind a wilted-up rose from my fifth grade graduation ceremony and a glass figurine of a sea turtle.

Practically invisible.

Not flashy enough for anyone to notice.

But it was something I'd loved almost my whole life—something that was worth more than money could buy.

Could I give it up forever?

I sat upright in bed and stared at it another moment longer before climbing down the ladder and moving toward the shelf. My heart swelled with excitement. Suddenly it didn't matter that it was one of my personal treasures and I'd have to practically destroy it to create something new.

Because all of a sudden, it wasn't mine anymore. Not really. It was Mrs. Taglioni's, and I just had to prepare it for her, make it perfect.

Maybe this was why I'd been safekeeping it for practically forever—for this very day, for my strange, old next-door neighbor who needed cheering up. I gripped it in my hand and my lips stretched into a smile. I had to get to work.

Suddenly I couldn't wait to see Mrs. Taglioni again.

Chapter 22

THE LEGEND OF THE TUXEDO PIGEON

I was five when Tom first told me about the Legend of the Tuxedo Pigeon.

We'd been playing in the backyard while Mom gave baby Amelia a bath. Tom threw a Nerf ball at Ellen, who in turn tossed it to Sarah, who then kicked it over Mrs. Taglioni's fence and started crying. After Tom climbed over the fence and got the ball, he told us he saw a Tuxedo Pigeon in her yard.

"What's that?" I remember asking him.

Tom's eyes were as big as full moons. "The Tuxedo Pigeon is a very rare and exotic creature," he said, bending at the knees to meet me at eye level. Even at thirteen, my brother seemed like a giant.

"Is it magic?"

"Very." Tom nodded. "The Tuxedo Pigeon has the power to change the color of its feathers. Legend has it that the bird blends in with the regular pigeons by turning itself brown. But, when the Tuxedo Pigeon has been called on a special mission, it turns its feathers black and white, so it looks like it's wearing a tuxedo suit."

"What kind of special missions?"

"All kinds," Tom said. "And usually they include fancy parties. That's why it gets all dressed up."

Sarah put her hands on her hips. "You're teasing."

I jumped up and down. "I want to see one!"

"Sorry, JoJo. It flew away as soon as it saw me coming. But . . ." He pulled a feather out from behind his back. It was an intricate black-and-white pattern that I'd never seen before, and the sight of it took my breath away. "It left this." Tom placed the feather in my open palm.

"Can I keep it?" I whispered.

"Yes," he whispered back.

"Do you think it'll come back again?"

Tom shrugged his shoulders. "Maybe after its special mission." Then he tossed the Nerf ball at Sarah. "Heads up!"

"I don't want to throw anymore," said Sarah, barely catching the ball before it clunked her on the shoulder.

"We'll kick it then," said Tom.

I sat down on the cool grass and spun the Tuxedo Pigeon feather between my fingers, careful to not damage it.

A magic pigeon.

I hadn't known such a creature existed.

I held on to the feather for years, a little piece of magic all to myself.

Until now.

Later that day, after we had secretly created presents for Handmade Christmas, gone to church, and stuffed our bellies with pizza, we gathered in the living room.

Still no sign of Mrs. Taglioni. Was she even coming over?

I *know* I didn't read her name wrong on that little piece of paper. I'd reread it a thousand times since that morning.

"I can't wait anymore," whined Amelia. "We always open presents on Christmas morning. And now Christmas is practically over!"

"It only feels that way because it gets dark earlier in the wintertime, so don't exaggerate," said Ellen, stretching out on the carpet. "And it shouldn't be a surprise that Christmas is a little different this year."

"It's almost time," said Dad from the doorway. He raised a cup of eggnog to his lips and smiled. "Just waiting on a few more people . . ."

Sarah sighed as if something was on the tip of her tongue, but she held her words back. Maybe she was excited for Handmade Christmas, too.

I bounced my knees on the couch. "Stopppp!" Amelia said. "You're shaking me."

"Sor-*ry*."

The doorbell rang, and Tom jumped up on his feet. He was football-fast to the door, swinging it wide open.

"Hiya, Lou," he said. "Dr. Stern."

"FINALLY!" Amelia zoomed to the hallway, and I followed at her heels to help hang their coats while Tom shut the door. "Look at all the snow on your boots!"

Dr. Stern laughed and tugged off her hat, sending a sprinkle of powdery-soft snow across the wood floor. "It's coming down fast out there," she said. "Hi, everyone! Thanks for the invite again this year. You know I can't pass up your mulled cider."

Mom smiled. "Of course! Your company is a Christmas tradition."

Dad turned up the radio in the living room as we all piled in, flopping on the couch and leaning on armchairs.

Dad checked his watch. "Should be any minute now . . ."

Amelia patted the floor for Sugar to stretch out by her feet, and I asked Mom if I could get Hamlet out of her Cave to join us.

"All right, honey. Just keep her under control, okay?"

"Promise, Mom!"

Just as I led Hamlet back into the living room, the doorbell rang. It felt like my heart did a somersault in my chest.

"Guess I'm the family butler?" said Tom, getting to his feet again.

"Well, at least you have *one* viable career option," said Ellen, rolling onto her stomach.

"Tom has *plenty* of career options," Mom said gently, raising her palm in the air.

"Not if he keeps changing majors," commented Sarah.

I looked at Mom. "You can change majors in college? I didn't know that."

"Of course, Josie. It's okay to have a shift in interests."

"Uh, hi, Mrs. Taglioni. Are we being too loud?" Although I couldn't see Tom in the hallway, the surprise in his voice was unmistakable.

The old woman cleared her throat. "Your father invited me. For Christmas?"

I've heard Mrs. Taglioni's voice all my life—from on the other side of the fence, while banging on our dining room wall, or rasping away about something at the front door, but I'd *never* heard it sound like this before.

It was shaky. Small. Higher pitched than normal.

Was Mrs. Taglioni actually *nervous*?

"Oh! Uh, can I take your coat?"

At least Tom found his manners! He emerged from the dark hallway, and Mrs. Taglioni slowly appeared behind him, giving the group an awkward half wave.

"Good evening," she said, patting her nest of hair. "Merry Christmas."

"So glad you could make it, Molly!" Mom gushed. "Won't you have a seat? Sarah?" Mom motioned for my sister to give up her prime spot in the leather recliner, and Sarah slowly slid down it onto the carpet like she wasn't quite sure what to make of our new guest either.

I wrapped my arms more tightly around Hamlet's neck. Hopefully Mrs. Taglioni wouldn't freak out over the pig. It's not like they had the best introduction. But I was glad Mrs. Taglioni was here, too.

"Hi, Mrs. Taglioni," I offered with a smile. She nodded in response as she sat down, clutching her handbag close to her chest.

"Angels We Have Heard on High" blasted through the speakers and Doug's tree lights twinkled in the corner. Once Mom and Dad were finished passing around drinks and German spice cookies and lemon squares, Dad clapped his hands together and said in a big, booming voice, "Kids, thanks for being patient today. . . . Your mom and I wanted to make sure this holiday was extra special, so we invited over a few guests." Dad turned his hand palm up and gave a grand gesture toward Mrs. Taglioni, Dr. Stern, and Lou. "Welcome to the first Handmade Christmas at the Shilling household!"

"At least he didn't say first *annual* Handmade Christmas," Tom joked in my ear. "There's still hope for next year!"

"Shhhh!" I hissed back, narrowing my eyes at him. "This is fun."

"Does everyone remember the rules—er—challenges?" Dad asked, and we all nodded. I noticed that Mrs. Taglioni seemed in agreement, too. Had she brought a recycled present for someone here? "Good." Dad grinned. "Looks like most of the presents are under the tree. But I'll walk around with this blanket in case you need to discreetly slip a gift beneath it. . . ."

Dr. Stern, Mrs. Taglioni, and Mom all pulled things from bags and slid them beneath the blanket, and then Dad covered the tree while he rearranged the presents underneath. When the blanket came down, it felt like curtains on a stage, and the show was about to begin.

Chapter 23

ROCKING AROUND THE CHRISTMAS TREE

Goose bumps sprouted across my arms. I glanced over at Mrs. Taglioni and watched as she adjusted her spectacles.

What if she didn't like my gift?

Mom passed the presents around. Most of them were messily wrapped with old newspapers, catalog covers, or recycled birthday wrapping paper.

"Youngest to oldest," Mom said. "Like always."

"Yay! Me first!" Amelia squealed, tearing at her gift. "It's . . . It's . . ." She unwound it, revealing two paper cups connected by a long cord. But it wasn't a cord— it was straws taped together, then with yarn wrapped around it. "A telephone!" Amelia exclaimed, raising a cup to her mouth. She tossed the other end to Lou and turned her cup around, pressing it against her ear. Lou whispered something on his end, sending Amelia into another fit of giggles.

"How're we supposed to know who it's from?" Sarah asked.

"Easy. It's Mom's yarn!" Amelia said. "Thanks, Mom!"

"Glad you like it." Mom's cheeks turned a light shade of pink, and it made me smile. I didn't know Mom was so creative. The handmade telephone was actually pretty cool. Maybe Amelia and I could attach it to our bunk bed and play with it later that night.

Lou's turn was next. It was one of Tom's old football jerseys, but with the sleeves cut off, so it looked more like the mesh pinnies we wore in gym class. "Awesome!" Lou exclaimed, pulling it over his head. The jersey was huge on his small frame, but Lou didn't seem to care. "We'll practice throwing this summer, right?" he asked my brother.

"Sure thing, buddy." Tom gave him a thumbs-up.

"I want to play, too!" said Amelia.

"Millie's super fast these days," I told everyone.

"Really?" Tom suddenly looked interested. "Spring

training is just around the corner, Millie. Maybe you should start doing sprints with me!"

"My worst nightmare," said Sarah, making a face and making me laugh. Running wasn't my favorite thing to do either.

"Hmm . . ." Mom glanced thoughtfully at my little sister. "Maybe there's a spring soccer league or something that we could look into for you, Amelia?" She winked at Dad. "It might be a good idea to channel all that energy."

My little sister grinned. "Really? Yeah, that'd be *so* fun!"

"Can I play, too, Mom?" asked Lou, looking up at Dr. Stern. She nodded.

"I think it's a great idea," she said, smiling. "Emily and I will see what we can find out."

"Awesome!" Lou and Amelia high-fived.

Dad motioned to me. "Your turn, Josie!"

"Okay." My fingers searched the gift in my lap. I carefully unpeeled the Scotch tape, unfolding the newspaper wrapping and revealing a book: *Charlotte's Web*. I blinked, confused. I hadn't read it in a long time because it was always tucked away with Ellen's books, but it looked the same as always, except—except for a bookmark, near the end. I flipped to the page and felt my heart swell and balloon, as if it was filled with more emotion than I could hold inside.

The bookmark was just a cut piece of white printer paper, but something was written on it: *Thought you could use some inspiration.*

I moved the bookmark out of the way, and my fingers paused on the scene when Charlotte the spider is sick but working hard to spin webs and save Wilbur's life at the fair.

In every place Charlotte's name was printed, a tiny piece of paper was carefully taped over it with the written name *Josie*. And where Wilbur's name had once appeared, it now said *Hamlet*.

I hugged the book to my chest. Tears filled my eyes as I made eye contact with Ellen. "Thank you," I said.

My older sister smiled. "You're welcome."

"That doesn't look upcycled," said Sarah, squinting her eyes.

I closed the book and placed it on my lap. Hamlet's eyes were fluttering closed, and her hairy pink skin was warm against my palm. "It's between Ellen and me," I said. "But it's perfect."

And it really was.

This book meant that Ellen recognized how important Hamlet was to me—and that she believed I had the power to save her life.

Suddenly, as I looked around at my big, wild family, I realized that they'd all been supporting me in different ways.

I glanced over at Sarah and remembered how it felt when she gave me the grips at my gymnastics meet. She had believed in me, too.

I watched as my siblings opened their presents, and when it was Tom's turn, I remembered the advice he'd given me earlier that winter.

The only one holding you back is you.

His encouragement had helped me focus in gymnastics and get past all my fears about being too tall and not as good as the other girls.

Even Dad! Maybe he didn't like Hamlet, but he protected her from Ms. Coburn's wrath. And although he hadn't seen my *first* back tuck at gymnastics, he had given me rides to and from practice and cheered me on at the big meet.

When it finally came time for Mrs. Taglioni's turn to open her present, I could barely contain my excitement. She studied her gift for a moment without saying anything. I had used an old *National Geographic Kids* magazine as the wrapping, making sure that the photograph of the sloth bear stretched across the top. Mrs. Taglioni's lips flickered with the hint of a smile as her fingers traced over the glossy paper. Then she carefully unwrapped it, revealing the Tuxedo Pigeon feather inside.

"What is it?" Lou asked, leaning closer.

Mrs. Taglioni's face twisted as she studied the end of the feather, where I'd remade it into something she could wear.

"A hair barrette," she said, turning it over carefully in her hand. Then she whispered in awe, "I once knew a bird with this coloring."

The old woman pulled a makeup compact from her purse, and while staring at the mirror, carefully pinned the Tuxedo Pigeon feather into her hair. She smiled—a *genuine*, happy smile—and looked around the room. "I'm afraid I don't know who this is from," she admitted.

My parents looked confused, but my sisters glanced in my direction. They knew as well as I did how long that feather had been in my possession.

I raised my hand, like I was in class. "Me. Um, me, Mrs. Taglioni."

"Well. Thank you, my dear." Then the old woman winked. "It's lovely. Now I'll always be ready for a *special* mission."

"Oh, yeah!" Tom snapped his fingers. "The Tuxedo Pigeon. I totally forgot about that feather. Man, I haven't seen one of those birds in ages! Remember, Mrs. Taglioni?"

My jaw dropped in surprise. "Mrs. Taglioni, you've heard of the Tuxedo Pigeon?"

"She's the one who told me about it," said Tom. "When I was a kid."

"I've not only heard about it," Mrs. Taglioni said, leaning forward. "I used to *own* one."

"Really?" Ellen held her face with her hands, leaning forward. "Will you tell us the story?"

Mrs. Taglioni shared how her younger brother used to attend exotic bird shows around the world, and that a long time ago, he brought one back for her. But they didn't realize at the time just how magical a Tuxedo Pigeon was, because most of the time it looks just like a normal pigeon.

"When it's called on a mission, its feathers change— and then nothing can stop it," explained Mrs. Taglioni, dancing her hands through the air as if a pigeon could fly into the room at any moment. "Not bars of a cage, or cement walls, or a closed window. *Poof!* Just like that, one day the Tuxedo Pigeon was gone."

"Did you ever see it again?" asked Sarah.

Mrs. Taglioni nodded. "It still lives around this neighborhood . . . somewhere. But it's an extremely busy bird, of course, and it really doesn't like cold weather."

"Is this for real, Dr. Stern?" asked Amelia, glancing at the vet.

"Quite," she said with a smile.

I stared at the old woman resting in the recliner, and it was like meeting someone for the first time. All these years—and memories—with Mrs. Taglioni in my life, and I'd never once tried to get to know her . . . I'd only judged her. And maybe she'd judged me a little, too.

Suddenly I couldn't hold back the tears any longer.

"Why're you upset, sweetie?" Mom asked, handing me a tissue.

"I'm not," I said, wiping my nose. "I'm just happy she likes the present."

And I was. I leaned in closer to Hamlet, and she nestled her snout into my wool sweater. It felt like the end of something, but the beginning of something else, too.

"And now for my gift!" Mrs. Taglioni said, reaching

into her purse. "But Josie may have to help me with this one."

She handed me a cube-shaped package wrapped in tin foil. It was labeled *Hamlet*. I tore it open, and Hamlet's nose perked up as a familiar smell filled the room. "I thought your pig and I could make up after that fence escapade," Mrs. Taglioni said. "A peace offering."

Homemade corn bread!

I gave it to Hamlet, who happily gobbled it up, licking every crumb she could sniff out on the blanket and floor.

"What a wonderful gesture," said Mom.

"That's so nice, Mrs. Taglioni!" exclaimed Amelia, and I nodded in agreement.

The old woman beamed as Hamlet closed her eyes and settled back into her cozy nap, happily full from the treat. "You know, my William loved pigs . . ."

"Who's William?" I asked.

"My late husband. He passed away many, many years ago."

"Oh . . . I'm sorry." I didn't know Mrs. Taglioni had ever been married, but I guess it made sense because she'd always been a *Mrs.* to me.

"It's all right, child. I have only fond memories."

She got to her feet just as "I'll Be Home for Christmas" began to play on the radio. "Now it's about time for this old lady to get to sleep. Merry Christmas, everyone. Thank you for the company this holiday."

"Merry Christmas!" everyone echoed back.

"Here, take some cookies home with you," said Mom, wrapping a plate in plastic wrap.

"Wait—" I stood up. "It's really snowing out there. I'll walk you home."

I grabbed our coats from the closet and swung open the door. A strong gust of wind swept into the house, and I helped shield Mrs. Taglioni from the falling snow as we walked down our stoop and up her front steps next door.

"Thank you, Josie," Mrs. Taglioni said to me as she unlocked her door.

"Merry Christmas, Mrs. Taglioni," I said, wrapping my scarf more tightly around my neck. We exchanged a smile and I added, "I'm glad you spent it with us."

Walking back to our stoop, I saw the lit-up Christmas tree and everyone in the living room through the big bay window. It was like watching one of those silent movies. Tom was doing some kind of hopping dance with chicken arms, and I wondered if the "Dominick the Donkey" song had come on the radio again, and Amelia was talking into her handmade telephone with Dad. Hamlet's front hooves were up on the windowsill, and she stared back at me from behind the frosted glass.

The city was so quiet, I could almost hear the falling snow over my beating heart.

Chapter 24

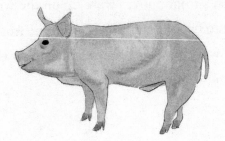

BRAINSTORM SESSION

I slapped another glossy poster onto a street pole, securing it with a piece of duct tape at the top. In bold, careful calligraphy, Carlos has written FREE PIG TO GOOD HOME and below it, Fernanda had used Photoshop to insert one of Lucy's photos of Hamlet.

Lucy held the roll of silver tape and scissors, cutting off a piece for me each time I needed it. "I know you're worrying," she said. "You always get quiet when you worry."

I put out my hand for another piece of tape but didn't say anything. She was right, of course.

"You'll find a good home for Hamlet soon," she assured me.

I nodded in agreement, but inside I wasn't so

confident. I only had a few days left before the New Year's Day deadline. And now it wasn't just my parent's deadline—it was the law.

"Have we gotten any emails yet?" I asked her. Since I didn't have a cell phone and Lucy did, she connected the email account we created to her phone so she could check the messages more frequently.

Lucy didn't meet my eyes. "Well . . ."

I stopped, rolling up the remaining posters into a big scroll. Something in my best friend's tone didn't seem right. "Well what?"

"I don't know if I should read it to you."

"Of course you should read it to me!"

"Don't say I didn't warn you . . ." Lucy sighed. She pulled her phone out of her pocket and tapped the screen until she pulled up the email. "Hi, Josie," she read aloud. "My friend saw your sign about giving away a pig. I might be interested. I live on a farm in Athens. How old is your pig? How much does it weigh? Please let me know ASAP because—"

She stopped. "Because what?" I said, hanging on every word.

"Because . . . my animals go to the factory in a few weeks. I could use the extra money and I'll give you ten percent of the profits," she finished.

Hearing those words made my stomach hurt. Hamlet. Going to a factory. No way—not on my watch. Not for a million dollars!

"I don't understand . . . pigs are so fun. Why doesn't anyone want Hamlet as a pet?" I slapped another poster onto a pole. Lucy handed me another piece of tape.

"Any luck with the animal shelters you called?" Lucy asked. "Oh—Carlos just texted. They're all waiting for us."

"None. And I've tried about a million." I sighed. "They all say the same thing. They don't take pigs, or they don't have space, and they refer me to some other place, and then they say the same thing. I feel like I'm on a merry-go-round of nos!"

My hope was deflating. We looped back to the Three Stoops, where I'd hung the pink bike chain ten minutes ago on the gate to call a meeting.

Sully was dribbling a basketball on the brick front step where he had shoveled off the snow. "I'm out of posters," he said in greeting. "Find a home for Hamlet yet?"

I shook my head. "We need to buy more time," I told them.

"We've got to think bigger than animal sanctuaries," said Carlos. His breath looked like a small cloud in the cold winter air.

Sully nodded. "That's what a detective would do. You know, think outside the box."

I tightened the scarf around my neck and sat down on the cold steps beside him. "Bigger *how*? Outside of the box—like outside of *Ohio*?"

Sully tapped his pencil on his notepad. "Forget animal sanctuaries. Who else would want a pig?"

"Not just any pig," said Fernanda. "A massive farm pig."

"A really slobbery hungry one," added Carlos.

"Farmers?" I exhaled. "But the only farms I can find online are businesses, like meat factories . . ."

"Did you ask your parents to help you?" asked Lucy.

I stuck my hands in my puffy coat pockets. "Mom made a few calls with me yesterday, but then she had to take Amelia to the pediatrician for a checkup. I've barely seen Dad at all lately, and everyone else is busy with finals." I sighed. "We're on our own."

"Hello, children," said a pleasant voice. We all looked up. Mrs. Taglioni was all bundled up with a black coat, furry scarf, and tall boots.

"Hi, Mrs. Taglioni," I said. I hadn't seen her since Christmas Day. My eyes fell on the Tuxedo Pigeon feather pinned onto the top of her hat, and it made me smile. "Where are you off to?"

"Catching a train," she said with a wink. "Even old ladies need an adventure sometimes."

"Sounds like fun," said Lucy. "I love riding the train!"

"Don't stay outside too long," said Mrs. Taglioni, wagging her finger. "They're saying more snow tonight!"

"*More* snow?!" Sully slapped himself on the forehead. "I'll be shoveling the stoop for the next week!"

Mrs. Taglioni laughed, and it made Sully grin. "Don't worry, child. There's a warm front headed our way on New Year's Day. All the snow should melt by then. Have fun and be careful!"

"Okay, thanks, Mrs. Taglioni," I said. "See you soon!"

Mrs. Taglioni waved good-bye. We watched her walk down the block, her boots crunching through the sidewalk snow, until she disappeared from sight.

"I want to take a train somewhere," muttered Carlos, opening a tin of colored pencils.

"We just got back from Thanksgiving in Chicago!"

said Fernanda with a laugh. "Anyways, don't forget Dad's taking us to see the ice sculptures in a bit, so quit your grumbling."

"You guys, I think Mrs. Taglioni just *laughed*! The world is coming to an enddddd!" said Sully, cupping his mouth with his hands.

"Very funny," I said. "She's actually really nice. Now back to Operation Home for Hamlet . . ."

Sully raised his pencil eraser in the air. "Okay. Only businesses are advertised in the yellow pages, right?"

I raised an eyebrow. "Yeah, so?"

"So you need to find a family—like normal people," Sully explained. "People who love animals as much as you do."

"Easier said than done," I said. "I mean, we have posters all over the neighborhood, and Tom posted it on his Instagram. He's up to like three thousand followers now, he said. And I asked Dr. Stern if she knew anyone who might want Hamlet. No luck!" I rolled back my shoulders.

Sully nodded. "You know, in the movies police always look for clues close to home. Maybe you should try that."

Cars whizzed down the slushy road, and I exhaled

again, watching my breath float and disappear into the thin, cold air. Closer to home? That was impossible. It was illegal to keep a pig in the city.

"You're getting quiet again!" said Lucy.

"You can't get frustrated," added Fernanda.

"Yeah," agreed Sully, trying to cheer me up. "You know what a cold case is? It's an investigation with no leads. And you know what? I think a good detective who thinks things through can always find a lead. You just gotta think outside the box."

Maybe Sully had a point. But I'd already asked Dr. Stern. And I didn't know anyone who had a farm. Everyone lived in the city in old townhouses like mine, or tall apartment buildings downtown.

Think outside the box.

Okay.

When was the last time I was on a farm?

"Well . . . Sarah used to take horseback riding lessons," I said. "It was a nice place, not too far away. Maybe I should call them."

Fernanda snapped her fingers. "Good idea! Horse stables at least have land and a barn and stalls . . . and they obviously like animals."

"Starburst?" Sully extended a palm.

"Sure," Lucy and I said, unwrapping the little square candies, while both the twins shook their heads. Sully shot me a knowing look, and Lucy continued, "What about goats? People who have goats probably like pigs. Maybe there's a goat farm around here somewhere."

"That's not a bad idea . . ." My mind spun, trying to think bigger, and I felt my heart begin to race, like how it does before a gymnastics routine. "Our school did a field trip to some historical farm last year . . . a place that was like frozen in time, back in the 1800s or something," I added. "They had a few animals roaming around."

"Oh, that's right!" Carlos grinned, looking up from his sketching pad. "That place was awesome. We got to milk a cow and wash sheep."

"It was soooooo gross!" said Fernanda, making Lucy laugh.

"I think we're onto something here," I said, suddenly feeling excited. I got to my feet and dusted snow off the back of my pants. "Thanks, guys! I'm going to make some calls now."

"Keep us posted!" said Fernanda. "Dad's taking us to an ice sculpture exhibit downtown, but we'll be back later."

"Yep," said Carlos, packing up his art supplies. "Good luck!"

"I'm coming with you," said Lucy, spinning the roll of tape on her fingers. "It's horrible when gymnastics is on break. . . . I get so bored being alone at my house while Mom and Dad are at work."

"We'll go hang more posters!" Sully gave me a thumbs-up, and I felt heat rise from my throat to my face, even though it was totally freezing outside and my cheeks had gone numb like five minutes ago.

"See ya. And thanks," I said, turning down the sidewalk before Sully could notice that he made me blush. Lucy jogged up next to me and flopped her arm around my shoulders.

"I saw that," she said with a smile.

"Saw what?"

"Your face got all red when Sully said good-bye to you."

It felt like flames danced across my cheeks. "No, it didn't."

"You can't fool me! I'm your best friend, remember? You like Sul-ly! You like Sul-ly!" she singsonged as we stomped up the stoop of my house.

"Shhhhhhhhh! And no, I don't."

Did I?

"Well. He likes you," said Lucy, shrugging.

My hand froze on the doorknob, and it wasn't because the metal was iced over. "How do you know?"

"Because he told me."

"What! Lucy!" I exclaimed, my eyes wide. "When?"

"Last week."

"And you're telling me this *now*?!"

"I know, it's totally been the hardest secret *ever* to keep!" Lucy grinned. "But I couldn't tell you until the gymnastics meet was over. So you could focus. Mind over matter, you know?"

I didn't know what to say. Or think.

Sully actually *liked* me?

My face burned again. I couldn't think about him now. I had other things to think about. I swung open the front door and was greeted with the warmth of the crackling fireplace in the living room across the hall. "Let's talk about it later," I said to Lucy. "We've got to find Hamlet a home." I kicked off my snowy boots. "We're gonna need a miracle . . ."

"Hey, if we can stick our Level Five routines, we can do anything, right?" Lucy said, hanging her coat on a wall hook. My heart raced as I glanced at the clock above the fireplace mantel. I wish I felt as confident as she did. "Oh!" Lucy peeled off her wool socks and tucked them in her snow boots. "And don't forget the gymnastics registration money is due on the first."

"Yeah," I mumbled, flopping on the couch and flipping through the yellow pages again. "I didn't forget."

One thing at a time, I breathed. I had phone calls to make.

Chapter 25

CRUNCH TIME

For the next two days, Lucy and I pored over the yellow pages and made phone calls during every free moment. We went to the library and sent emails to our local politicians, requesting a change to the livestock law. We asked our principals to send out an email to the schools' listservs, and since I didn't have a Facebook account, I asked my older siblings to post our digital flyer on their pages. We taped more posters to utility poles around the neighborhood and printed out another batch so Fernanda, Carlos, and Sully could pass them out to their friends and families also.

Then I begged my parents to help me. Mom searched online message boards for leads with me at the library one afternoon, and I even overheard Dad calling a few of his friends, asking if anyone might be interested in adopting a pig.

No luck.

With every passing day, Hamlet gained another pound. I thought she was massive a month ago—but she was a downright *dinosaur* pig now and ate practically as much food as Tom!

I had to hand it to Dad, though. He hadn't complained about Hamlet in . . . I don't know when. And now that she was way too big for her Cave beneath the stairs, he let her roam the house. Hamlet mostly followed Sugar everywhere she went and slept in front of the fireplace, but when we ate meals, she bullied her thick body past our legs and sat beneath the table, ready to scarf up fallen food.

Okay. *Sometimes* I snuck her food off my plate. But I wasn't the only one! Even though Dad didn't realize I saw him, he slipped Hamlet green beans under the table the other night. And you know what? Dad didn't even reach for the hand sanitizer afterwards!

There were a few times I wondered whether we could just secretly keep Hamlet. No one would really notice, right? It's not like the mayor was driving by our townhouse every day making sure the livestock law was being followed.

But I stopped wondering after *the call* happened.

At first when I heard the man say, "Hello, Josie?" I thought it was Lucy's dad's voice. But I was totally wrong.

"Yes?"

"It's Officer Brady. Do you remember me? I checked on your pig awhile back, with Officer Chou."

It felt like I stopped breathing. It was three days before New Year's Day—Deadline Day for Operation Home for Hamlet. We still had time! So why was he calling?

"Hi, officer," I said, twisting the phone cord around my finger. "Yes, I remember."

"Do you still have livestock on the premises?"

I puckered my lips. What a horrible word: *livestock.* It reminded me of the way I felt when Dad didn't want me to call Hamlet by a name, back on Thanksgiving, because it'd make me get attached to the pig.

Well, I *was* attached now. And maybe Hamlet was livestock or whatever, but she was also *my* pet pig until a nice family decided to adopt her.

My gaze shifted down the hall where Hamlet was

stretched out in front of the fireplace on top of Dad's blue slippers. "Yes," I admitted. "Hamlet is still in our house. But we still have three days left—"

"Good news," he broke in. "We found a home for your pig. They'll pick her up on December 31st."

"Wait—what?" I shook my head, like I was some remote control that didn't work right.

"They've got a pickup truck and a crate, so your parents will just need to be on-site to oversee the transfer, but luckily they're off the hook with transportation. Does eight o'clock work? Will someone be around, even though it's a holiday weekend? The man might call you to coordinate the details, but I wanted to give you a heads-up."

Was this good news, or bad news? I wasn't sure.

I swallowed hard, choosing my words carefully. "Officer Brady, I just have a few questions, okay? Who is this person?"

I heard a shuffle of papers. "Hmmm. A man named Grimson. Like the color crimson, but with a *G*. First name Reggie."

"Where does he live?"

Officer Brady paused, like he was squinting to read tiny handwriting. "Let's see . . . about thirty miles outside the city. He's got fifty acres of land. That's bigger than most city parks, you know. Sounds like it's for his kid to take care of? Oh, and he'll pay you market price, too."

"Market price?"

"A hundred bucks. That's the going rate for a pig her size, gender, and age, apparently."

"He's going to *pay* us for Hamlet?" I felt frozen in place. I didn't know what to say, or what to do, so I just whispered, "I—I don't know about this, Officer Brady. Can I meet him first?"

The policeman sighed. "Listen, kid. I know this must be real hard for you. I had some strange animals as pets when I was your age, too. But if the livestock remains in your home on the first of the year, animal control is scheduled to come and pick her up—then her future will be out of your hands and you'll have to face the judge for city violations. Take the hundred bucks and let the pig go, okay?"

It felt like her future was out of my hands *now*, but I didn't say that out loud. Instead I just nodded and said, "Yes, officer. Is—is Mr. Grimson a nice man? He likes pigs?"

I heard a phone ringing in the distance. "I've gotta

take this call now. Yes, yes, I'm sure he's great. Reggie Grimson. December 31st—eight o'clock in the morning. Happy holidays!"

"Um. Happy holidays."

Click. The phone's dial tone buzzed in my ear for another moment, and then I hung up the phone, stunned.

This was a good thing.

Wasn't it?

Someone with a farm wanted Hamlet—and they were willing to pay for her, too. A hundred dollars didn't quite cover my gymnastics registration fee, but it was pretty close. . . . I'd have a better chance of convincing Mom and Dad if we had some extra cash to pay for it.

This should be a win-win. . . .

So why didn't it feel like one?

I ran my hands through my hair, trying to quiet my worrying mind. But I couldn't, no matter how hard I tried.

Hamlet was going to have a new owner, and his name was Reggie Grimson.

Who *was* this guy?

I had to find out, and I knew just the person to help me with research.

Chapter 26

DOWN FOR THE COUNT

Sully was waiting on the library steps by the time I arrived. "Sorry I'm late!" I said, stomping the muck off my boots. Mrs. Taglioni was right—a warm front did sweep through the city, and the once-white snow was now all dark and slushy. "I had to walk Hamlet and Sugar, and Hamlet flipped her water bowl, so all her newspapers got soaked. . . ."

"No problem. The library closes in an hour, so we'll need to hurry." Sully slung his backpack over his shoulder, and we entered through the revolving glass door. As we walked through the main lobby, Sully whispered, "Are you sure about this?"

"Sure about what?" I whispered back.

"You know . . . checking into this Grimson guy."

"Sully! I *have* to find out who's taking Hamlet."

"Shhhhhhhh!" An employee stopped reshelving books from a cart and raised a finger to her lips. I mouthed *Sorry!* and motioned Sully over to the computer room.

Once the door shut behind us, I saw we were the only ones in here. Good. We could talk without bothering anyone. I glanced over at Sully, who tossed his Lakers backpack and navy coat down on an empty chair, and felt my face turn red again.

I was alone with Sully!

Suddenly, even though we'd been friends and neighbors for ages and ages, I felt nervous. Thank goodness he didn't seem to be. Sully got to work, logging onto a computer with his library card bar code.

"Okay," he said, leaning toward the computer screen and looking serious. "Operation Home for Hamlet is in full effect. Let's check criminal records first."

"You can do that?"

"Sure. That's what Google is for. . . . What'd you say his first name was?"

"Reggie," I said, pulling up a chair beside Sully and trying not to think about my shoulder touching his.

Sully opened up a new browser window. He could

type like a billion words a minute! In no time we were looking at a search page. *Click, click, click.* "No strong leads . . ." Sully said, squinting his eyes as we scanned through the search results. "I don't think this is right. Everyone is online. It's called a Digital Footprint. This Grimson guy is MIA."

I breathed a sigh of relief. "Well, maybe it's a good thing?"

"Maybe," Sully said, but his knee started bouncing, like he was trying to shake off a thought. "He could have an alias, though. Happens all the time in the movies."

"A fake name?"

"Yeah."

"Hmmm . . ." I snapped my fingers. "Try Reginald. That's probably his real name anyways."

"Good thinking!"

Sully typed *Reginald Grimson* into the search bar, and a banner reading NO RESULTS flashed across the computer screen. "Do you have his phone number?" Sully asked. "If it's listed, we can double-check that with public records to see if the number matches his name."

I shook my head. "I didn't get it. . . . Officer Brady

said he might call us later. But if this Reggie guy calls the home phone, we don't have caller ID. If he calls Dad's cell, it's going to be hard to get that number without looping my parents in. . . ."

We sat there, thinking. Finally Sully looked over at me and said, "Want to come to one of my basketball games sometime?"

I practically jumped out of my seat. "Oh! Um, that would be fun," I said, trying to keep it cool.

"I think I found something!" Sully sat upright. "Here we go. Grimson's Gables. There are photos, too."

I squeezed my eyes shut. "I'm too nervous. I can't look!"

"Okay, okay . . . It looks nice, actually. . . . There's a lake, and a big brown barn, and chickens. Oh, wait."

"What?" I peeked out of one eye. Sully quickly exited out of the window browser. "Sully—what's wrong?! You're freaking me out here."

He adjusted his baseball cap and turned to face me. "Josie, this Grimson guy can't take Hamlet."

"What do you mean? What was on the website?"

Sully's face had gone pale. "That guy, Reggie? He's a hog farmer, Josie. Trust me. Hamlet's *not* gonna be a pet."

A dark silence filled the computer room. I leaned back in my chair and stared at the ceiling. We'd raised Hamlet from a little piglet to a fiesty big pig. I'd grown to love her wild, curious personality, and over these last couple months, she'd become part of our family.

I'd promised her a good, long life.

And now I'd failed her.

Over the loudspeakers, the librarian announced, "This is just a friendly reminder that the library is closing in twenty minutes."

"What're you going to do now?" Sully whispered.

I looked at the wall clock. It was almost five o'clock— practically dinnertime. Reggie Grimson was going to be at my house in less than three days. He had our address and phone number and Officer Brady's contact information and everything.

There was no time left to *do* anything.

I needed to think bigger, but I didn't know how anymore.

"I don't know, Sully," I said, sliding my arms into the sleeves of my winter coat. "I honestly don't know."

Chapter 27

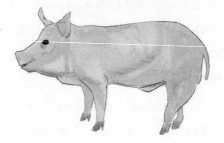

INSPIRATION STRIKES

Later that night, I was stretched out on the floor of my bedroom, hunched over one of Sarah's horse magazines looking for a potential home for Hamlet, when Mom knocked gently on the bedroom door.

"Honey?" she said. "Can I come in?"

"Sure."

"We missed you at dinner." She entered the room, and it filled with the smell of spaghetti with marinara sauce. "I brought you a plate."

My stomach growled, but I was too upset to eat. "I'm not hungry."

"Why don't I just set it here in case you change your mind." Mom lay down on the floor beside me. "Do you want to talk?"

I shook my head. "There's nothing to talk about."

"I know how attached you are to Hamlet. Why not spend this evening with her, instead of cooped up in this room? Dad grilled an ear of corn for her and chilled the two halves in the fridge. Would you like to give her one as a special treat?"

"Because . . . I can't bear to look in her eyes," I admitted, and Mom's face fell.

"Oh, sweetie. I know you're worried about Mr. Grimson, but your father spoke to him on the phone today. I think he plans on giving Hamlet to his daughter. He was happy to hear that Hamlet got along well with dogs. It sounds like Hamlet will have lots of new friends."

I felt myself start to panic. "Mom, Mr. Grimson just can't take Hamlet. He *can't*!" My chin began to tremble. "That man's lying! Hamlet will be *you know what* before Valentine's Day."

Mom's lips pursed together. "I'm afraid there's no other option, sweetie. You gave Hamlet such a good life here, making her that cozy Cave, and you did such a wonderful job of taking care of her. I'm really proud of you. And I know that she's special to you but, sweetie, it's time for Hamlet—and our family—to move on now, okay? It's best for her to live on a farm." She pushed the plate toward me and got back on her feet. "You'll feel better after you eat something. And if you change your mind, I'll save that ear of corn in the fridge. It'll be there when you want to give it to Hamlet."

I said nothing when Mom left the room and closed the door behind her. I just stared at the firefly twinkle lights hanging in our bedroom, and I didn't speak to my sisters when they came up to bed. Amelia tried to talk to me on her handmade telephone, but when she pressed a cup up against my ear, I only held it and listened.

Don't be sad, Amelia whispered.

All I wanted to do was head downstairs and wrap my arms around Hamlet's neck and tell her everything was going to be okay. But I couldn't. She was a smart pig. One look into my eyes, and she'd know that I failed her.

I let Amelia's telephone cup fall from my ear and climbed up the rungs of the bunk bed ladder, curling into a ball beneath the covers. Tears stung my eyes, and I didn't bother holding them back anymore. The harder I cried into my pillowcase, the heavier my body felt.

"Josie?" said Sarah lightly. "Do you need anything?"

I didn't answer. It was hopeless.

I slid my hands beneath my pillow, rolling to face the wall. One of my sisters switched off a lamp, and the room fell into darkness. My fingertips grazed something rigid beneath my pillow: a book, and my reading flashlight.

I slid beneath my patchwork quilt, flipped on the light, and opened up Ellen's copy of *Charlotte's Web*, the present she'd given me on Handmade Christmas. The bookmark my sister made stuck to the inside pages. I peeled it off and read her cursive handwriting again.

Thought you could use some inspiration.

I wiped away my tears and began to read. I started with my favorite parts first, like when Wilbur first met Charlotte the spider, and how she rattled off the names of body parts, totally grossing Wilbur out, and then flipped forward to when Charlotte weaves words into her web, and the Zuckerman pig becomes world famous.

I slammed the book shut. *That was it!*

I slipped down the bunk bed ladder and tiptoed over to Ellen's lower bunk bed. It was almost pitch-black in the room, except for a single butterfly-shaped night-light that glowed along the wall.

"Pssssst! Ellen!" I whispered, pressing my fingers into her forearm.

Her eyes fluttered open. "Josie, what *is* it? I have to be up at five for my paper route!"

"I need your help," I said, barely able to contain my excitement. Maybe, just maybe, I could pull this whole thing off and Hamlet actually stood a chance.

"Do you actually *know* people at the paper?"

Ellen rubbed her eyes. "Yes . . . why? What is it?"

"Like, do you know any reporters who might be interested in a story?"

She reached for her eyeglasses on the nightstand. "Okay, what's this about?" she whispered. "Is everything all right?"

I fell to my knees, feeling more desperate with every passing minute. "I need to talk with someone at the paper tomorrow," I whispered, so as not to wake up Sarah and Amelia. My eyes began to adjust to the darkness, and I saw Ellen's eyebrows pinched together in worry. "It's urgent," I continued. "But I need your help, too. I have an idea. Will you help me? Before it's too late?"

I wasn't making much sense, but I was so tired and worried that I couldn't quite form the words the way

I was thinking them. Ellen stared into my eyes for a moment, not saying anything. Then, softly, she whispered, "Is this about Hamlet, Josie?"

A knot formed in my throat. I couldn't speak. The sun would be up soon, and then it'd be my very last day with Hamlet ever, ever, *ever*, unless I came through and saved Hamlet's life.

"We're her family, whether she stays with us or not, and family is family! I want to do something—something big—to save her life. But I can't pull it off without your help. And Sarah, Amelia, and Tom, too. Please?"

"You've never asked me for my help before."

There was the hint of surprise in Ellen's voice and maybe a little sadness, too. When *was* the last time I'd done something alone with Ellen? I couldn't remember. We barely talked these days. I figured she thought I was this annoying kid sister who she had nothing in common with. . . . But maybe she'd been feeling left out lately, too.

"I'm asking you now," I said. "Help me distract Mom and Dad in the morning so I can loop the bike chain at the Three Stoops and call a meeting. And I need my siblings there. Please?"

My older sister's lips curled into a slow smile, like

she was proud of me but wasn't quite sure how to say it. She reached for my hand and I knew she was in.

"Get some sleep, Josie," she said, giving me a squeeze. "Tomorrow's a big day."

Chapter 28

TICK TOCK

It was the biggest meeting ever held at the Three Stoops. My three sisters squished together on the red-brick steps, alongside Lucy, the twins, and Sully, while Lou and Tom leaned against the front gate. The sounds of cars cruising down the street and kids gossiping on the stoop filled our ears, until finally I clapped my hands together to bring everyone to attention.

"I know you're all wondering what's going on," I said, standing tall in the sunshine. "But I realized something important last night about Operation Home for Hamlet. All these phone calls and posters? People aren't connecting because they don't *care*. Those animal sanctuaries and horse farms probably talk to a hundred kids a day about a hundred other pigs. They're tired of the same old requests over and over. Hamlet means nothing to them. But she means the world to *me*. If people care about Hamlet like I do, they're more likely to help her. We need to show people how special she is."

Sully's face lit up. "You're right!" he said, raising his pencil to his chin. "Hamlet needs buzz."

"Totally." I nodded. "We need to think through all the things we love about Hamlet so we can spread her message far and wide. Sully, write these down!"

"She's really sweet," began Lucy. "She's always licking my hand, even when I don't have snacks to give her."

"She's curious," said Ellen. "Remember when she opened the fridge by herself? She's a very intelligent animal."

"And she's super nice to Sugar," Amelia pointed out. "She loves snuggling with her in front of the fire."

"I think it's cool that her tail curls and uncurls when you scratch her back," added Carlos.

"She's getting better at catching the Frisbee," chimed in Lou. I noticed he was wearing the upcycled gift of my brother's old football jersey.

"Hamlet can catch a Frisbee?" said Tom. "Awesome."

"Yeah!" echoed Amelia. "She got four out of ten tosses yesterday. Hamlet's *super* athletic. Maybe you could play Frisbee with us sometime?" she said, looking up at my brother.

"Sure, Millie! After we do sprints," Tom said, giving her two thumbs-up. "I need to see that speed I've been hearing about."

"I like how Hamlet closes her eyes and just relaxes when you give her a warm bubble bath," said Sarah, redirecting the conversation.

I turned toward her in surprise. "You've given her a bath? I thought you didn't like Hamlet!"

"So maybe I bathed her a *few* times when you were at gymnastics practice," Sarah said, shrugging. "And *maybe* it was sort of fun. I blame PSAT studying for a brief lapse in sanity."

Ellen laughed. "Oh, I don't think you can blame it *all* on the PSAT," she said, elbowing Sarah playfully.

I grinned at the sight of my two older sisters getting along. "Okay everyone, this is a good start. So, here's my idea about what to do next . . ."

Once I ran through the plan, everyone started talking at once.

"We could make a website, too," suggested Fernanda. "I know all about that from my girls' technology club. We've been learning coding."

"I've got new photos and videos to send you!" said Lucy, pulling out her cell phone and tapping through her albums. "I have the cutest photo of Hamlet sleeping next to Sugar. . . ."

"What if we made, like, a movie trailer to put on the website, too?" Fernanda continued, her voice rising in excitement. "Maybe we could post it on Facebook to help get the word out. Or YouTube?"

"I'm not allowed to have accounts until I'm thirteen," I told them. "But maybe you guys would share it?" I looked at my older siblings.

"Ah, yes, that's where I can come in," Tom said. "Social media is my specialty. Gonna be verified on Twitter reallllll soon."

"Sure you are," Sarah said, laughing. "No problem, Josie. We can definitely help spread the word online."

"Maybe my mom could post something on her clinic's website, too?" Lou suggested.

"Good idea!" said Amelia.

I turned toward my older sister. "Ellen, can you place an ad in the paper to run in tomorrow's issue?"

"I think I can pull a few strings." She winked. "I've been with the paper a long time. Maybe they'll even do it for free."

Sarah leaned against the brick foundation of the townhouse. "We're going to need a lot of supplies to make this happen, guys," she said. "And I know *just* the place to find them."

Amelia's eyes lit up. "Maybe Doug can help out, too! He doesn't need his lights anymore."

"He did a good job this Christmas, that Doug," sighed Tom, stretching his arms over his head. "I'm not ready to say good-bye to him."

Sully looked up from his notebook. "Who's Doug?"

"Our Douglas fir," said Ellen and Sarah at the same time.

"Jinx!" cried Amelia.

"Okay, okay." I laughed, cracking my knuckles. "Stoops crew, if you all handle the computer stuff today, the Shillings can take it from there."

"Tonight, after Mom and Dad fall asleep, you can count on us," Tom said. "I might need someone to wake me up, though." He grinned sheepishly. "I tend to sleep through alarms."

"Another one of your specialties?" Sarah elbowed him.

My brother grinned. "Bingo."

"Yep, don't worry, Josie! We've got the website covered," said Lucy, wrapping her arm around Fernanda's shoulders. "Easy peasy."

I felt my spirits lift. Hamlet still had a chance. Even if it was a small one, it was *something*. I wasn't going to go down without a fight, and I had my friends and family to help me.

That night, Ellen set her alarm for 1:00 a.m., so we could get started when our parents were fast asleep. When she tapped my shoulder and said gently, "Josie! Wake up!" I bolted upright in bed and met my siblings for our secret meeting in the living room.

"Who's brewing the coffee?" joked Tom, running his hands through wild hair.

"Don't you dare touch that coffee grinder!" I warned him. "You'll wake up Mom and Dad and ruin the whole thing!"

He laughed. "Kidding, kidding . . ."

"There's no time to lose, shortcake," whispered Sarah, motioning toward Mom's craft closet. We grabbed old yarn and ribbon before combing through the downstairs bathroom cabinet for cotton balls. Then Sarah retrieved a stuffed plastic bag, hidden behind the fridge.

"What's that?" Ellen asked.

"Payday supplies," Sarah said, pulling out the biggest

bag of cotton balls I've ever seen.

"Sarah! This is amazing!" I cried, giving her a hug.

"Good thinking," said Ellen, and Sarah grinned.

"This is quite touching, but I'll get started with unwinding Doug's lights," said Tom, rolling his eyes. "Come on, Ellen, I need your help." The two oldest kids worked on taking down the Christmas tree lights while the rest of us started on Hamlet's Cave.

Even though she was much too big for it now, Hamlet still ate her food and drank water beneath the stairs, and the overhang of the stairway was the perfect spot for our masterpiece.

My eyes grew heavier with each passing minute, but cutting through scrap paper and stretching out cotton balls and doing it all with my siblings by my side somehow made me feel stronger.

We worked until two in the morning, and Hamlet's Cave transformation was complete. After we were done and everyone drifted off to their beds, I barely slept a wink, lying on the couch with Hamlet and Sugar resting on the floor, staring into the twinkling Christmas lights now decorated across the stairwell, hoping that some of Tree Day's magic still lingered in the air.

Chapter 29

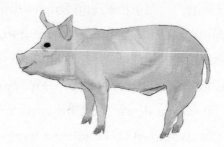

HAMLET'S WEB

Before anyone woke up, I cleaned up the mess from last night, started coffee brewing for my parents, and microwaved a frozen pumpkin waffle. And then I waited until floorboards overhead creaked, listening for the sound of footsteps on the stairs.

I led Hamlet back to her Cave, and we sat down.

"Josie?"

Dad stood at the bottom of the stairs, wearing a bathrobe and his favorite blue slippers, and rubbed his eyes. His eyes darted from me, to Hamlet, and then to everything us Shilling kids had made.

I moved toward Dad, handing him a steaming cup of black coffee, and admired our work. It felt like I was seeing it for the first time, even though I was exhausted and worried and still a little bit hungry, too.

Twinkling Christmas lights framed the scene, like a giant painting. Twisted, colored pipe cleaners arched across the hallway. Tissue streamers fluttered down from the ceiling, flanked by two dangling fly swatters that were attached to old plant hooks. Mounds of cotton balls, stretched thin and wide, created a massive web above us. Carefully, in the center of the web, a red velvet ribbon spelled out one single word in delicate cursive.

Heart

"Josie, what is this?" Dad said in awe.

"Hamlet's Web."

"You *made* all this?"

"We all did," I said, nodding toward the ceiling, where my sisters and brother slept upstairs. "Just like Charlotte."

Dad's eyebrows softened, erasing the crease across his forehead. "Josie, I—" Dad started, but then Amelia slid down the banister screaming, *"Wheeeeeeee!"* before collapsing into a pile at the bottom of the steps.

"Morning!" she said. "Wow! It looks even better in the daytime!"

Dad stared at the web. "How did you girls even *reach* that high?"

"Stood on a chair. *Sometimes* being tall has its bene-fits." I laughed. "Besides, having Tom around is like having a ladder handy."

Suddenly the whole house erupted in noise. Sarah was yelling about a missing sweater until finally Ellen admitted to borrowing it, to which Sarah didn't even get mad or anything, she just said, "That's fine." Mom called downstairs asking about the morning newspaper, and Sugar barked at the back door, wanting to be let out.

Dad took another sip of coffee. "Josie, I know today's going to be a hard day for you. It's a beautiful thing you all did for Hamlet, honey. I'm so proud of you. Let's take a photo so you always have it, okay? Why don't you and Hamlet go stand beneath the web."

I nodded, leading Hamlet over to her Cave and wrapping my arms around her neck. Dad clicked off a few pictures.

"It's almost eight," I said, checking the clock in the kitchen. My nerves were beginning to set in. *What if the plan didn't work?* "Will you get everyone together while I take her outside? So they can all say good-bye to Hamlet?"

Dad nodded. "Sure, sweetie."

"Okay. I'll be with Hamlet and Sugar out back for a bit," I said, heading toward the back door and overhearing Mom exclaim from the bottom of the stairs, "Oh my goodness, would you look at this!"

Time seemed to move forward in slow motion. With every passing minute, I felt anxiety brewing in my stomach, and it was so much stronger than I'd experienced from gymnastics.

At eight o'clock on the nose, we heard the sputter of an old engine out front. I raced to the bay window and pulled back the curtains. A man had double-parked an oversized pickup truck on the street. There was a giant metal crate sitting on the bed of the truck.

He flipped on his flashers so that the city traffic would pass him in the other lane. I glanced over at Ellen, who was sitting on the couch with an open book. She met my eyes. "No one else is here," I said, feeling my words catch in my throat. "It's too late. It didn't work!"

I felt my heart rate skyrocket. The doorbell rang. Dad smoothed his palms on the front of his jeans and opened the door wide.

"Hello, you must be Reggie Grimson," Dad said. "I'm Stephen Shilling and this is my wife and children—"

"Good morning," I heard him reply. "Is the pig in a crate somewhere?"

Mom cleared her throat. "No, we don't keep her in a crate. She lives in the house with us. In her cave."

"Cave?"

I imagined Dad's face turning red as he explained, "Under the stairs."

I rounded the corner and finally got a good look at Hamlet's new owner. In my mind, Reggie Grimson was going to be this big, scruffy guy, wearing denim overalls and chewing on a piece of hay. But he couldn't have been more different.

Grimson wore a crisp suit, as if he'd just left a breakfast business meeting. Behind him stood a big guy wearing a long T-shirt and jeans, clutching a choke collar and long chain leash in one hand.

My heart began to race. This wasn't happening how I'd planned! I backed slowly down the hall toward Hamlet's Cave and carefully linked my thumb between her leather collar and the hairy skin of her throat. There was no way she was going home with this Grimson guy. We'd sneak out the back door and run down the block if we had to!

"Would you like a hot cup of coffee?" Dad asked.

"We just brewed a pot. Our family would like the opportunity to get to know you better; as I'm sure you know, we're quite attached to Hamlet."

"Double-parked," said Grimson, motioning out to the truck. "We'll just take her and go, if you don't mind. We have other collections on the agenda this morning."

"Collections?" Mom raised an eyebrow. Dad also looked taken back by his words and tone.

"Josie? What's going on?" Tom said from behind me. I spun on my socks. He must've just finished showering. His longish hair was wet and slicked back, and he was wearing a button-down shirt and khakis, like he was headed to church.

"Mr. Grimson is here." His name felt like poison on my lips.

Tom grimaced in disapproval. "And where is—"

Dad stood there like a stone statue, blocking Mr. Grimson from entering the house, but also not closing the front door at the same time.

I understood that uncertainty about what to do next. If Hamlet stayed in the house, someone from animal control would come pick up Hamlet tomorrow anyway, and the government would give my parents a massive fine and a citation breaking the law.

But if Hamlet left with Reggie Grimson . . .

My sisters watched from the living room with wide, worried eyes. Mom moved to stand alongside Dad, widening their human wall. Tom edged closer to me and patted Hamlet's head reassuringly.

I swear, my heart beat so loudly it echoed throughout the whole house.

And then it happened.

Chapter 30

LIGHTS, CAMERA, ACTION!

A bright light shone into the house, and a solid red light caught my eye. It was a video camera!

"It is here, in a small townhouse in the busy Northeast neighborhood, where a farm pig has stolen the hearts of many," said a soft but firm voice. A tiny woman with hair combed into a tight bun appeared in our doorway, squeezing between Grimson and his employee. The microphone and light followed her, and a cameraman came into view. "Evette Waters, reporting live from the scene, as this domesticated creature is about to be removed from the city limits and transferred to her new, legal abode . . ."

My heart soared. *Was this really happening?!*

"The oldest son, Tom, saved a runt piglet from

slaughter, and it is here where the pig found refuge . . ."

"What's going on?" Grimson grumbled, lifting a palm to block the bright, artificial light from his eyes.

"I have no idea—" Dad started, but Tom called out, "Here I am! I'd be happy to answer your questions!" My brother popped the collar of his shirt and strode down the hallway.

Evette leaned the microphone his way. "Tell us, Tom," she said gravely. "Take us back to that moment on the farm."

Tom pressed his shoulders back. "She was a small, scrawny piglet, not much more than bones, and her littermates had edged her out of the way. The farmer was going to put an end to her life, so she didn't suffer from starvation. But that's where I stepped in. I hid the piglet in my football helmet, took her back to my dorm room, and the rest is history."

My brother was a natural in front of the camera!

"You're a hero!" she gasped. Tom flashed my parents an *I told you so!* look. "How do you feel about the pig's destiny now?" she continued. "It must be *so* difficult for you . . ."

"Hamlet leaving is hard on all of us," said Tom. "But you know, it's really my little sister, Josie, who's been affected the most—"

"Ahh, yes! Josie Shilling! Let's hear your thoughts on the matter." Evette Waters pointed the microphone toward Sarah.

"*I'm* Sarah," my sister said, motioning to me. "*That's* Josie."

I squinted under the camera light. Everyone stared at me. I felt Hamlet tense beneath my hand, and I stroked her back to calm her down.

"And there's the pig! Look at the two of them now," she said warmly, "Let's zoom in on this, Eddie—"

This was it—Hamlet's moment to show the world how special she is. But to do so, I'd have to walk by Grimson and his man. What if they just grabbed her and took off?

I glanced at Dad. A reassuring smile passed over his lips. "Go on, Josie," he said.

I breathed deeply and exhaled.

It was go time.

Hamlet and I walked down the hall, her hooves *clip-clopping* on the wood floors. Evette smiled at me, and by the twinkle in her eyes, I knew she wasn't just here for the story—it was because she cared.

"It's okay, Hamlet," I said, scratching her behind her

ears right at her favorite spot. Then I looked into the video camera lens and said, "We've got something to show you."

I brushed past Mr. Grimson and his sidekick, leading the group down the front stoop, where a small crowd had gathered on the sidewalk, curious about the big truck and television crew van in front of our townhouse. I noticed orange cones blocked off the street, and Officers Brady and Chou were rerouting cars to the next block over.

I looked down the block, and Sully, Carlos, Fernanda, and Lucy stood on the twins' stoop next door. They all had big smiles plastered on their faces, and when I met Lucy's eyes, she gave me two thumbs-up.

Ignoring the camera crew focused on us, I leaned down and gave Hamlet a big hug around the neck. "You know I think you're the best pig in the whole wide world. You don't need to prove anything to me," I whispered in her twitching ear. "But there's a whole lot of people needing to see it to believe it, so here's your time to shine." She oinked softly back, and it felt like an understanding of some kind.

Amelia waited patiently about ten steps out, a bright yellow Frisbee tucked under her arm. "Ready?" I asked her. She nodded and handed off the Frisbee to Lou. I loosened my grip on Hamlet's collar.

"Ready!" I yelled at the top of my lungs. "Set! GO!"

Lou released the Frisbee. It soared through the air into a high arch. Amelia sprinted down the block, past the Three Stoops, around the standing crowd, and suddenly Hamlet took off after her, galloping to keep up.

"Oooooo!" I heard a passerby call out. "There's a *pig*!"

"GET IT, HAMMIE!" Amelia shouted as the Frisbee began to descend. The pig catapulted on her hind legs, jumping high into the air and catching the yellow disc in her mouth, before landing gracefully back on her hooves.

"Awesome!" Tom shouted from behind me.

Amelia did a fist pump in the air. The Three Stoops crew cheered, and Sarah whistled. I pulled half an ear of corn out of my pocket—the grilled one Mom had made the night before—and Hamlet came trotting right back to me, dropping the Frisbee and chomping down on the corncob.

"That was amazing," Evette breathed. "You got all that, Eddie?" The cameraman nodded, a big grin on his face. Even Mr. Grimson looked slightly amused.

Hamlet was a star!

"What else can your pig do?" the reporter asked.

"Open the fridge!" said Amelia, skipping up the front steps.

"Jump a fence," added Dad, who winked at me.

"Use the litter box," said Mom.

"Climb a bunk bed ladder," I added, to which Ellen and Sarah snapped their heads to my attention and exclaimed, "What?" in unison.

"Amazing. A pig that does tricks!" Evette adjusted her tortoiseshell glasses and faced me again, her expression turning somber. "Josie, how do you feel about giving your pig away today?"

"Well, we aren't really *giving* her to Mr. Grimson," I said. "We didn't know about it until recently, but there's a livestock law in the city, which means you can't have farm animals living within the city limits. For a long time, I wanted to keep Hamlet here, with us, but . . ." I sucked in a deep breath and exhaled. "I've realized that the law is in place for a reason. Hamlet deserves a long and happy life at a farm, where she can roam freely and have animal friends. That's all I want for her now."

"Ah, yes—Hamlet!" Evette clapped her hands together. "What a brilliant name."

"My idea!" chimed in Tom.

"If you're just tuning in, the website to learn more about this city pig is flashing across the screen at this very moment, and use hashtag #SaveTheCityPig to share your thoughts with us online now!"

"What is this website?" Mom asked, raising an eyebrow.

"The Unlikely Story of a Pig in the City dot com!" Evette cried. "The video of this sweet city pig and her story has gone completely *viral*."

I grinned. The Three Stoops gang came through after all!

"Viral, huh?" Tom's face lit up.

"Now, Josie," Evette said, swinging the microphone in front of my face, "what are *your* hopes for the family pig?"

"Hamlet's part of our family now," I said, motioning toward my parents, my brother, and three sisters, who grinned back at me. Ellen gave me a thumbs-up. "We just want her to be happy."

"Oh, would you *look* at that." Evette reached for my hand, and suddenly we were walking toward Hamlet's Cave together. "Eddie, get this, get this. The Shillings built a web, just like in *Charlotte's Web*. Well, I never ... Isn't that sweetest thing? Josie, come here, come here, tell me about this—What does that word say? In the web?"

"Heart."

"Ahh, yes. Heart." Evette nodded. "What a beautiful word. Tell us about that, will you?"

"There are so many words to describe Hamlet, and what she means to me . . . " I reached over and swept back the fine hairs on her neck with my palm. Hamlet rubbed her snout against my T-shirt, making me laugh. "She's smart and fun, and sweet and curious. But what I love most about Hamlet is her heart. She's got so much love to give. I just want everyone to know that."

"How touching. And Reggie Grimson . . . *You*, sir. What are your intentions with adopting the pig?" Evette moved toward him, sticking the microphone right by his mouth, leaving him no choice but to answer.

"I'm not *adopting* the pig." Grimson's lips twitched. "It will join the rest of my stock. Now if you'll excuse me, we need to—" He grabbed the chain leash from his employee and started toward Hamlet.

"No!" I cried, pulling Hamlet close.

"Not so fast," said Mom, a spark in her voice. "You said Hamlet was going to rustle behind cattle on your farm—that your daughter would be in charge of caring for her."

"You're a pig thief," I said, wrapping my arm protectively around Hamlet's neck. "See Mom? Dad? I told you. He's not going to keep her for a pet. It was all a lie."

"He's a robber!" cried Amelia.

"He's a *hamburglar*!" yelled Tom, fist pumping in the background.

"Listen, I don't want any trouble," Grimson said. He knelt down to talk to me, the way grown-ups do sometimes when they *really* want you to listen. "Look at the size of this pig, kid. You think it's a pet? Oh, no, this isn't some domesticated potbellied pig breed on your hands. You've been hoarding a massive Tamworth in the city! That's a prime *bacon* pig. Now. We're both reasonable people here. On the phone, your parents said I was doing you a big favor. You're breaking the law aren't you, trying to keep this pig? You don't want to break the law, do you?" Grimson pulled out his money clip, peeling off three crisp hundred-dollar bills. He stuffed them into my palm and curled my fingers over them. "Here. Take the money. That's well over market rate for a Tamworth sow. It's time to let the pig go and move on."

I looked down at the money in my hand. This was a lot of cash—money that could pay for gymnastics next year. But there wasn't a dollar amount on my love for Hamlet, and I knew that deep in my bones. I glanced at my parents. Mom nodded reassuringly and Dad's lips pressed into a tight smile, and I knew they were both on my side.

"I'm sorry for your trouble, Mr. Grimson, but the deal's off," I said, tucking the crumpled bills into Grimson's shirt pocket. "Hamlet's staying. You can go."

I heard Evette Waters gasp, pushing the foam-covered microphone a little closer to Grimson. He stared at Hamlet for another moment. Then he looked around at each member of my family, then the television crew, and down at Hamlet. He sighed loudly and finally walked off toward the truck.

"And there you have it, folks," Evette said into the camera, relief sweeping over her face. "Live from the Northeast side, Evette Waters here asking you to consider pet adoption! If you or someone you know wants a *wonderful* pet pig"—the camera zoomed in on Hamlet's face, and the reporter wrapped her arms around her neck—"call this hotline number on your screen *now* and visit the Unlikely Story of a Pig in the City dot com!

Not a moment to lose, or the pig will be snatched up by animal control tomorrow. Let's save this pig from Hog Heaven together!"

As if on cue, Hamlet licked Evette's cheek. The video camera's red light shut off, and Evette and her cameraman gave their final good wishes before racing out the door to cover a traffic collision a few blocks away.

We all stood there in awe of what just happened.

Did Grimson really just leave?

Is Hamlet actually staying?

And were we just on television?!

I reached into my pocket and gave Hamlet the other half of her corncob. She munched it loudly in the hallway as Mom crouched down at the front doorstep, picking up today's issue of *City Centennial* off the welcome mat.

"Josie, did you see this?" Mom said, handing it to me.

I shook my head, taking the paper in my hands. A black-and-white photo of Hamlet was on the front page, just above a lead article with the headline: CITY PIG FACED WITH HOG HEAVEN.

"They printed the story," I said in disbelief. I looked up at Ellen, and she was grinning from ear to ear.

"Must've been a slow news day," deadpanned Sarah.

"This is amazing!" Mom said, taking the paper back from me and unfolding it.

"I want to read the article!" said Amelia, reaching for the paper.

"You know how to read?" joked Tom, and Amelia gave him a playful shove.

"*And* I can Google."

"No one's Googling anything," Dad said with a smile. "Unless it's Hamlet's website. Is the library open today? We need the internet."

"Ahhh, music to my ears, Dad," Tom said.

Sarah smirked. "So, about that . . . I might've hacked into Mrs. Taglioni's Wi-Fi next door."

"*Sarah!*" Mom scolded.

Dad gave me a hug. "I'm proud of you, Josie," he said. "You did the right thing, turning down Mr. Grimson's money. It wouldn't have been right to let Hamlet go with him. I understand that now."

"They even mentioned how Hamlet is litter box trained!" Mom said proudly, skimming the front page article. "We'll have to frame this." She carefully folded the newspaper back up and motioned to the massive, colorful web in the stairwell of the house. "Josie, I still can't believe you did all of this!"

"We all did it," I said. "We're a team."

Hamlet brushed against my jeans, looking for a back rub. I knelt down beside her and stared into her eyes. "You're some pig," I whispered to her. "The best pig ever."

I was still scared, but for once, I felt at peace, too. I'd done everything in my power to save Hamlet's life. Now I just had to wait and see if my plan worked.

Then I looked at my family. "Do you think anyone will learn Hamlet's story and want to adopt her? Before tomorrow's Deadline Day?"

"I'm not sure, Josie," said Dad, sweeping a hand through his graying hair. "I guess we'll just have to wait and see."

We didn't have to wait for long.

The house phone began to ring.

Chapter 31

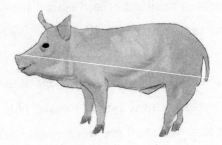

NEW YEAR'S EVE

It seemed like everyone in the world wanted Hamlet.

Okay. Maybe not everyone, but all the right people, and that's what mattered.

Turns out, the hotline number flashing on the screen during the news broadcast rerouted phone calls to our house line. All in all, eight people rang us that day wanting to adopt Hamlet, and Lucy received sixteen emails from the website contact form.

Sixteen!

Gathered around the speakerphone, we got to ask each family questions about where they lived and what Hamlet's new life would be like, and why they were interested in adopting her. Everyone seemed really nice. They didn't make me feel ridiculous when I mentioned that Hamlet's favorite foods were made with corn, or how she loves belly rubs, and that I swear she can read your mind sometimes just by looking into your eyes.

We were on the phone for hours it seemed. My throat was sore from talking so much, and my brain was tired from thinking through all the options. But my heart felt *full*.

It was late into the evening, just as we were gathered around the family table for fondue with carrots, apples, and sourdough bread, that the final call came through. A call that I would never have expected in a million, trillion years.

The call that changed everything.

His voice had a familiar quality to it, even though I'd never met him before. He was kind and knowledgeable about pigs—even the Tamworth kind, which is what Mr. Grimson said she was—and *very* familiar with Hamlet's story.

It felt right.

No. Not just right.

Perfect.

Later that night, my family was sprawled out in the living room and we talked over the options. It smelled like a movie theater in the house, all buttered popcorn and root beer. Deciding on Hamlet's new family had to be unanimous. Hamlet was special to all of us, and we each got a say in the matter. Tom and Ellen even canceled their New Year's Eve plans so we could all be together tonight to figure things out.

But in the end, it wasn't a hard decision. Like Sully told me once, sometimes the answer is closer to home than you might think.

After watching *The Sound of Music* and before the New Year's Countdown specials on television began, Dad said he had an announcement.

"Are we getting a new car?" Amelia guessed.

Tom kicked his feet up on the ottoman. "If you get a new car now that I'm out of the house, I might cry."

"No one's crying. And we're not getting cable," Dad said, laughing. "And the van has another twenty thousand miles in it, I think." He moved to stand in front of the room. "Well . . . here goes. I got a new job."

We all gasped.

"Were you fired?" I asked, feeling my cheeks blaze with heat. "Does this have to do with Hamlet and the dinner with your boss?"

Dad shook his head. "No, Josie. This has been a long time coming and has nothing to do with Hamlet. After eight years with the same company, I was ready for a new challenge and a different employer. I start on Tuesday!"

"Wow, Dad, congrats!" said Tom.

Sarah's face suddenly drained of color. "We're not moving, are we? I'm a junior, guys. We can't move right before my senior year—"

"No, we're not moving," said Dad, smiling. "We're happy here." Then he looked around the room. "Aren't we?" We all nodded. It might be hard being a big family living in a small city townhouse, but this was our *home.*

"Does this mean no Handmade Christmas next year?" asked Amelia.

"We'll figure that out when the time comes."

"Cuz it was fun . . . and I really like my telephone."

Mom ruffled her hair. "That warms my heart, Millie."

I snapped my fingers. "I get it now! *That's* why you've been at the library so much lately and having all those phone calls and late meetings. You've been interviewing!"

"I had to brush up my résumé. And I didn't want to say anything until a position was finalized," Dad said, and then he cleared his throat. "Listen, kids. I know it's been a tough few months for all of us. I just want to thank you for hanging in there and let you know that things are going to get better, okay?"

"I'm proud of you, Dad," said Ellen. "Congrats!" Tom gave Dad an air high five, and the rest of us clapped. Dad looked a little embarrassed, but he smiled all the same.

"And . . . there's something else . . . drumroll please . . ." Mom pounded on the coffee table with her palms, and Dad laughed. Another surprise? I sat upright. "We're getting internet!"

"HOORAY!" Ellen cheered, and Amelia jumped up on the sofa in happiness.

"Guys, I just moved out—you're killing me!" said Tom, splatting his face with his palm.

"Good timing, because Mrs. Taglioni changed her Wi-Fi password, and I wasn't sure when it'd be appropriate to ask her for the new one," said Sarah with a sly grin.

"Does this mean I can get Facebook now?" asked Amelia.

"*No*," said Mom and Dad in unison.

I snuggled up with Hamlet and Sugar in front of the fireplace and laughed while my brother tried to teach

Ellen how to swing dance, something he'd learned at a football fund-raiser event. Sarah flipped through *Young Rider* magazine, reading an article on Shetland ponies and tearing out the horse posters inside for Amelia, while my Dad sipped hot chocolate and my Mom set out Tom's championship football trophy on the mantel.

The New Year's Eve ball seemed extra shiny tonight. The energy in New York City was so electric, it radiated from the flashing television screen into our cozy Midwest townhouse living room.

The countdown to midnight began.

10

9

We sat upright, staring at the TV screen in excited silence.

8

7

The television camera pulled back from the crowd of faces, lifting high into the night sky. There were like a trillion people squished together, all screaming and clapping and jumping up and down, and even though it was so late at night, the city was *alive* with colorful lights.

6

5

4

3

We all jumped to our feet. Almost time!

2

1

The sparkly ball dropped, its bulbs glowing in bright white, dazzling the crowd. A rock song blasted through the speakers. Everyone cheered. Confetti fluttered around Times Square, and Amelia tossed construction paper snowflakes over our heads, calling out "Happy New Year! Happy New Year! Happy New Year!"

It was Deadline Day.

I scratched Hamlet's belly and she snorted loud, happy snorts. For the first time in weeks, my insides weren't pretzled up in knots, and I wasn't afraid to go to bed, fearing what New Year's Day would bring.

Because now I was ready.

Hamlet oinked in my ear, and I knew she was ready, too.

Chapter 32

NEW YEAR'S DAY

Before we left the city on New Year's Day, I paraded Hamlet down the block on a leash for the last time. Everyone had a chance to say good-bye. Lucy cried, Fernanda gave Hamlet a peeled banana, Carlos sketched her picture, and Sully snapped photos of her sitting on the Three Stoops.

"I'm going to miss you, Hammie," wailed Lucy.

"We can visit her as much as we like," I reminded her. "Plus you'll be busy with gymnastics."

Lucy gave me a look. "You mean, *we'll* be busy with gymnastics."

"Um." I swallowed hard. "I'm not sure I'm going to be on the team again."

"Wait. *What?*"

I took a deep breath. Now was the time to tell Lucy about something Dr. Stern mentioned to me that day we were cleaning the clinic. I wasn't quite sure how to talk about it, because I hadn't decided what I was going to do yet.

"Dr. Stern offered me a part-time job helping out at her veterinary clinic after school," I explained. "It's a lot of cleaning cages in the beginning, but maybe I'll learn about how to care for the animals, too." I shrugged. "Who knows, maybe one day I'll be a veterinarian, just like her?"

"But I'll miss you so much," Lucy said, frowning. "And you're so *good*—"

"Thanks," I said. "But you know what? It might be nice to try something else for a while and see how it goes?"

Something had changed in me this winter. Having Hamlet at the house helped me realize that gymnastics was just *one* piece of my life. There were other pieces to me and other things I might like. For once, the idea of putting my energy into something else wasn't scary.

It was kind of exciting.

"That's great, Josie," said Fernanda.

"Do you think Dr. Stern will let me visit the clinic to

draw the animals?" asked Carlos.

"I don't see why not!" I said.

"And the Three-Week Rule comes true again!" said Sully victoriously, his face smug.

I laughed. "Oh, yeah? How's that?"

"You just think about it and get back to me." Sully grinned, and I couldn't help but grin back.

Maybe I *did* have a crush on Sully!

"Okay," I said, my mind spinning.

Could Sully actually be right? Did the Three-Week Rule *really* exist? When Dr. Stern gave Hamlet a physical exam back around Thanksgiving, I knew I'd always liked animals . . . but it wasn't until that day on Mrs. Taglioni's stoop after Ralphie died, when Dr. Stern mentioned that animals seemed to like me, too, that I started noticing it more and more. And before I knew it, all kinds of things were swirling around my brain: good things—not just fears about my gymnastics routines or me growing too tall, too fast.

"Can't you do both, Josie?" Lucy sighed. "Gymnastics *and* work at the clinic?"

"I don't think so." I shook my head. "But I haven't decided for sure what I'm going to do yet, okay?" Dad honked the horn on the van as he pulled in front of the

Three Stoops. I tightened my grip on Hamlet's leash. "Gotta go, guys."

"Bye-bye, Hammie!" Lucy said, giving the pig one last hug. "See you soon! I promise to visit!" Sully, Carlos, and Fernanda did the same, and I led Hamlet down the stoop steps.

"Hey, Josie—I have a basketball game tomorrow! JUST SO YOU KNOW!" Sully yelled out from behind me. I glanced over my shoulder and caught Lucy's eyes widen like, *What's that all about?*

Sully's hands looked frozen on the rim of his baseball cap. It felt as if my heart was soaring in my chest, and I couldn't help but grin back. The world felt like it was in slow motion for one minute, and I said, "I'll be there," and grinned back.

Leading Hamlet toward the van, I waved good-bye to my friends.

"Ready?" asked Dad when I swung open the door. The family was piled in the three rows. Hamlet jumped up and squeezed her big body into the far back by Tom, like she was just another one of the kids.

"Yep," I said, buckling my seat belt. "Let's go."

Chapter 33

HOME SWEET HOME

It was the warmest New Year's Day on record. At least, that's what Lucy said Evette Waters reported on television that day. By lunchtime, most of the snow had melted away. The sun was radiant, giving the winding country road a shiny glow as we whooshed past farm after farm.

"This is it," Mom said, tapping the map in her lap. Dad slowly pressed the brake pedal, and we all peeked out the left window at a long driveway. The property was tucked away behind tall pine trees and a rolling hill, so we couldn't get a good look at it.

The van tires crunched on the gravel as we drove up toward the house, curving alongside a pasture of grazing horses and a few cows. We parked in front of a large red barn. The doors had been pulled wide and windows swung open. Chickens pecked for grain by a water trough.

None of us spoke a word as we got out of the van. I kept Hamlet on the leash for now, just until we were sure everything was right as rain. We walked up to the house, and it was like every single one of us wanted to soak it all in: the smell of wet soil and grass, how it felt in your lungs to breathe in the cool, crisp air. Hamlet's chin lifted, and she bobbed her snout a few times, as if she caught wind of something exciting about to happen. My heart swelled, and I rubbed her back. "I feel it, too," I whispered.

The man was waiting on the steps, just as he said he would be. "Hi there," he greeted us, smiling. "Happy you made it!"

Even from a distance, I could see wrinkles on his face. He had the same dark, frizzy hair like his sister, but he was nearly bald on the top of his head.

"We're glad to be here," Mom said. "I'm Emily. This is my husband, Stephen, and our five children, Tom, Ellen, Sarah, Josie, and Amelia. And of course, this is Hamlet!"

He took a few steps in our direction. "Nice to finally

meet you. I'm Mike Upton." The screen door behind him opened wide and slammed shut. "That must be Molly now . . ."

Mrs. Taglioni greeted us with a warm smile. Her black-and silver-speckled hair had been unpinned from her usual high bun, and it flowed in curls past her ears. "Hello, everybody," she said.

"Hi, Mrs. Taglioni!" I called out.

"Saw you on the news. You're my famous neighbors now!" Mrs. Taglioni said, loosening the scarf around her neck. "Warm out, isn't it? And Josie, I had no idea the pressure you were under regarding that pig. . . ." She shook her head. "Fresh corn bread just out of the oven. Who wants some? Children? Hamlet?" She winked.

"Me!" said Amelia and Sarah in unison. Mrs. Taglioni passed the plate around and gave an extra big corn bread square to Hamlet, who gobbled it up on the front yard.

"I can't tell you how grateful we are, Mike, that you're willing to adopt Hamlet," said Dad. "Josie gave her a bath this morning, so she's nice and clean."

Mr. Upton led us to the barn. "I'm glad it worked out. I have a soft spot for animals. But I think my older sister might've told you about that . . ."

"We heard about the bird shows!" said Amelia,

making Mr. Upton laugh again.

"I want to hear more about them," added Ellen.

"That was a long time ago when I was a more adventurous sort," he said. "But I did go to *quite* a few bird shows. Now here we are." Mr. Upton stopped in front of a fenced pen attached to the barn. A pile of fresh hay sat beneath an awning, and several troughs provided fresh water and food scraps. "My donkey used to live in this pen before she died last year, and nothing would make me happier than Hamlet moving in." He motioned to the doors. "It's got inside and outside space, so she'll be free to move around as she pleases."

"She'll like that," I said, scratching behind her ears. Hamlet tugged hard on the leash. I laughed. "I think Hamlet wants to take a look around."

"Smart pig," said Mr. Upton. "Here you go, Hamlet. Welcome home."

Hamlet had a makeshift cave at our house, and now she had a real deal pigpen. Mr. Upton opened a little gate and let Hamlet inside while he told us about the other animals on his property. I immediately liked the soft tone of his voice and the way he talked about his animals' personalities like they were part of his family. Hamlet sniffed around for a bit and guzzled down

carrots before plopping down in a pile of mud and rolling around. We all laughed.

I'd given Hamlet countless baths over the last few
months, but I'd never seen her face like this before.
I swear, Hamlet was actually *smiling*, if that was even
possible!

Chipmunks and birds darted in and out of the pen,
fluttering around the cedar chips in search of leftover
food. There were two big food bowls that Mr. Upton
assured me were heavy and designed just for mischie-
vous pigs who like to flip their bowls.

"She's going to fit right in here," Mr. Upton said,
hooking his thumbs on his belt loops. "And my grand-
kids sure will be happy to have a pig around!"

I grinned. We had learned about Mrs. Taglioni's
brother during our phone conversation yesterday. He
was divorced, had three grown children and ten grand-
children. Mr. Upton said his door was always swinging
open and closed with visitors popping in to take the
horses on trail rides, feed bread to the ducks, and make
s'mores out by the fire pit. And when he told us that
Mrs. Taglioni took the train out every month to visit
him, I almost couldn't believe it. She had this whole
other life I had known nothing about!

"Don't worry, Hamlet will get lots of attention," Mr. Upton said. "And remember, you're welcome to visit any time you want."

"Maybe we'll take the train out together sometime?" Mrs. Taglioni offered. "It's always nice to take a train ride."

It was then that I remembered seeing her the other day when I was hanging out at the Three Stoops, and how Mrs. Taglioni wore the Tuxedo Pigeon feather pinned on her hat. She had told us she was off on an adventure—and she was! She came to her brother's farm. It was here that she saw my family on the news with Evette Waters and learned about the trouble we were in, trying to find Hamlet a home. She had talked it over with her brother, and they both agreed that Hamlet should come live here, with Mr. Upton and his animals.

And that's when the call came through—the call that changed everything.

I never would've guessed that Mrs. Taglioni of all people would be the one to help us find a forever home for Hamlet. But sometimes in life, the answers to your greatest questions are right there in front of you.

I leaned against the fence, watching as the chickens pecked in the dirt and Hamlet stretched her legs out.

We stayed and had lunch with Mrs. Taglioni and Mr. Upton, and then it came time for good-byes at the barn.

Everyone had his or her chance to say something to Hamlet. Tom recounted the story about when he first saved her life, and Dad finally laughed about all of it, retelling our chaotic Thanksgiving to Mr. Upton and Mrs. Taglioni. Mom shared the story about Hamlet's Escape, and Ellen added how I gave all my allowance money to pay for Mrs. Taglioni's fence, which made the old woman rush to my side and give me a hug. Sarah laughed about the awkward dinner with Ms. Coburn, which made Dad sigh in relief that his new job was starting soon. Amelia recounted the day Hamlet raided the fridge while she tried to defend it with a fly swatter and told Mr. Upton that he'd better not install floor tiles in the barn because Hamlet likes to pull them up with her teeth. Then everyone looked at me.

"What will you miss most about Hamlet, Josie?" asked Mom.

I stared at the pigpen for a moment, thinking about it. There were so many things I'd miss about Hamlet—a trillion things I'd never forget. But there was one thing that I'd been thinking about that whole morning.

My eyes welled up with tears. "How she made us

feel like a family again."

"Oh, honey." Dad gave me a squeeze. "We're always a family."

"I know." I nodded. I *did* know. Mom smiled.

"Yeah, you can't get rid of me, sis," said Tom, elbowing me in the ribs and making me laugh. "Even if I *am* at college."

"Or *when* I go to college," said Ellen.

"Same here," said Sarah.

"Or me!" chimed in Amelia, raising a mittened hand.

"Now, before we head home, I have one final thing for Hamlet . . ." Dad said, popping the trunk of the van. He pulled out his favorite blue slippers. "Just something for her to remember us by." Dad tossed them on a bed of straw in Hamlet's Pen and then turned to my brother. She immediately nuzzled her snout up against them, happy as can be. "And Tom? We love when you come home for visits, but no more pigs, okay?"

Tom nodded. "You got it, Dad. No more pigs."

"Or earrings," added Sarah.

"Or laundry!" said Ellen.

"When can I get my ears pierced?" asked Amelia, making Mom laugh.

"C'mon, kids," she said. "Let's go home." Everyone

started to pile in the old van, but I stopped just as Dad climbed behind the wheel.

"Dad?" I said. "Can I have one more minute?"

It felt like I'd said good-bye to Hamlet a hundred times already, but I needed to be alone with her. I walked toward the fence and leaned against the wood. The clouds parted, and sunlight filled her pen. Hamlet's eyes half closed. Her soft oinks sounded light. Happy.

This was right.

And this wasn't good-bye.

"See you soon, Hamlet," I said, trying not to cry. "I love you."

I blew Hamlet a kiss, and she oinked back, as if she knew we'd be together again soon. As I walked toward the van, I didn't look back.

But a rustle in the nearby trees made me look *up*. A black-and-white bird rested on a twisted branch. It spread its wings wide and took to the sky, making me gasp out loud. I swung open the van door, calling out to my family, "You won't believe this, but hurry! LOOK! LOOK!"

I pointed, but the blue sky was empty except for drifting clouds. But I knew—deep down inside—that I didn't imagine the magical Tuxedo Pigeon. It had been on the farm. And now it was off on its next mission.

"What is it, Josie?" asked Ellen.

"Oh, nothing, I guess," I said, sliding into a seat beside Sarah.

Mom smiled. "You okay, sweetie?"

I nodded, staring out the window as Dad turned the ignition and started to drive. My heart had never felt so full before. There were so many changes happening at once.

How could someone be so sad and so happy at the same time?

But I was also something else.

I was thankful.

We listened to music and played games on the drive home. By the time we parked in front of our tiny city townhouse, I didn't feel like crying anymore. Sure, it was like a piece of me was missing with Hamlet back at the farm, but I had a whole life here with my friends, and maybe gymnastics, or possibly helping Dr. Stern out at the clinic. And who knows? Maybe I'd even have a boyfriend one day, too.

Plus, I had my big, wild family. And I wouldn't change that for the world.

ACKNOWLEDGMENTS

It is a difficult task to properly thank all the incredible people who not only bring a book to life, but who have supported you on your creative path.

Thank you to my rock star literary agent, Alexander Slater, for making my dream a reality and guiding me on my debut publication journey. I'm forever grateful to you and the whole team at Trident Media Group.

To my fabulous editor, Jocelyn Davies, thank you for loving this story as much as I do. Your smart, thoughtful edits made it infinitely stronger. You are a dream editor, and I'm extremely grateful for the support this debut has found at HarperCollins Children's Books. It takes a whole bunch of talented people to publish a book, and I'm deeply thankful for everyone's hard work copyediting, designing, marketing, publicizing, and selling my first novel, with an extra shout-out to David Curtis for the cover design and to Pascal Campion for the cover art. Thank you!

I wouldn't be the person I am today without all the wonderful teachers, administrators, booksellers, and librarians who provided me with safe places to read all sorts of books and ask questions about them, who taught me how to read, how to listen, and how to write. Special thanks to everyone at Jones Middle School and the Upper Arlington Public Library in Columbus, Ohio. To Mr. Dom Forker, my Del Val High School English teacher, your Creative Writing class changed the direction of my life. To FSU Professors David Kirby and Barbara Hamby, thank you for teaching me the value of a workshop. To poet Luci Tapahonso, my U of AZ MFA thesis advisor, thank you for your kindness and gentle mentorship. Christine Tomalin, I have never forgotten your kindness and guidance—thank you.

The initial inspiration for this book was Ellie, an actual piglet that was the runt of a litter, and the story of how my brother, Rich, saved her life and brought her home from college (the *Columbus Dispatch* even wrote an article about our family and Ellie back in 1994). Thank you to Ellie; Rich; my sisters, Renda, C, and Leslee; my parents, Richard and Carol; and all the extended family, too, for the variety of ways you've supported my creative endeavors. And a big heartfelt thank-you to the Kendalls—Glenn, Donna Jean, Pam, Deb, and the whole crew—for your love and encouragement through the years.

To the National Geographic Channel Digital Media Team, past and present—Matt, Brad, Skye, Alison, Leslee, Ashley, Meghan— thank you for nurturing my writing career in its early stages, and for letting me share about Ellie the Pig on the Nat Geo Wild platform. Thank you to Dr. Steen Bech-Nielsen, the veterinarian who cared for Ellie back in the day when he was Professor in Public Health and Swine Disease at the Ohio State University, for recounting your pig examinations to me via email so many years later, from half a world away. Enormous appreciation goes out to Club Champion Gymnastics in Pasadena, California, for allowing me spend time with a Level 5 team, and thank you to former gymnasts Theresa Galbo and Ashley Ludwig for feedback on gymnastics scenes.

I owe tremendous gratitude to Molly O'Neill, who nurtured the narrative of Hamlet and Josie in its infancy. Thank you to illustrator Katy Betz and Storybird for providing a very early version of this story with a platform and beautiful community. And an outpouring of love for E. B. White—thank you for writing *Charlotte's Web*, which will always be one of my all-time favorite books. It still gives me goose bumps that our two pig books share a publishing home.

Many scenes from this book were written and revised on the road. Thank you to Muscoot Farm in Westchester County, New York, for permitting me to hang out with the pigs. Big thanks to Petunia the Pig at M3 Acres and the Mulieri family in Redding, Connecticut, for letting me film and photograph Petunia's behaviors (and all those piglet hugs, too). And cheers to Tusk & Cup Fine Coffee in Ridgefield, Connecticut, for fueling me with bagels and coffee during my year of revising this book.

To the Society of Children's Book Writers and Illustrators, I was forever changed when I joined your membership a decade ago. This is important work, and I'm eternally grateful to be a part of such a wonderful, welcoming organization.

To my Write Nite ladies—Kim Liggett, Bridget Casey, Kristi Olson, Bess Cozby, Rebecca Behrens, Gabriela Pereira, and Michelle Schusterman, with an extra hug to my long-time SCBWI critique group partners, Alexandra Alger, Gina Carey, and Ghenet Myrthil—thank you for the community. Special thanks to Kate Messner for answering a variety of questions during my debut year, to Jay Asher for your encouragement through the years, and my agent sister Dana Langer for your friendship.

To the Class of 2K17, other 2017 debuts, and the YA Muses, thank you for the privilege of being part of your ranks.

As a child of God, thank you to Jesus Christ my Savior for loving me and saving me by grace alone. To my Redeemer MMG and WMG ladies, your perspective is a wonderful reminder of what's truly important in this world. Big hugs to my oily community,

#TheGoldenDropSociety, Lesley Graham, Ashley Cribb, and Heather O'Dell. I'm honored to call you dear friends (and I'm forever in your debt because, Peace & Calming).

I'm lucky to have a wonderful circle of friends. So much love for Meghan Barbieri, Erika Baylor, Karina Kuhary, Amanda Goetz, Jeannine Williams, Rebecca Smith, Emily Williams, Charlotte Addison, Heidi Browne, Jamie Chaft, Heather Linden, Meredith Stinnett, Jenica Patterson, Holly Marfani, Jennie Major, Meredith Maclaine, Julie Hanson, Vicky Roh, Lauren Oursler, Lisa Brininstool, Andrea Kwiatkowski, Adrienne Langbauer, and Emily Borell—thank you for all the encouragement.

To Leslee, I don't know what I'd do without you. Thank you for being my first reader since the beginning, and for never doubting that all my wild, ambitious writing dreams could come true. This book is for you.

To Bobby, thank you for all the times you've listened to me brainstorm, read my early drafts, sent me off on surprise writing retreats, bought me books, cheered on my successes, acted as my pocket thesaurus, loved me despite my many, many flaws, and lifted my spirits from the sadness of failure. I love you forever. I couldn't have done this without you. 24601.

To Townes and Lennox, I love you both so much. I hope this story makes you proud of your old mom.

To my readers, thank you for opening up this book and spending time with Josie, Hamlet, Lucy, Mrs. Taglioni, Dr. Stern, all the Shillings, and the Three Stoops crew. I hope you enjoyed it. You, dear reader, are why I wanted to become a children's book author. Thank you for allowing me the best job in the world.